P9-DFO-680

APPLEWHITES
AT WIT'S END

Also by STEPHANIE S. TOLAN

APPLEWHITES AT WIT'S END

STEPHANIE S. TOLAN

HARPER

An Imprint of HarperCollins*Publishers*

Library of Congress Cataloging-in-Publication Data
Tolan, Stephanie S.
Applewhites at Wit's End / Stephanie S. Tolan. — 1st ed.
p. cm.
Summary: Great changes are in store for the highly creative
and somewhat eccentric Applewhite family when money
problems force them to open a summer camp for gifted children,
who almost immediately begin to rebel, while a mysterious
interloper watches from the woods.
ISBN 978-0-06-057938-8 (trade bdg.) — ISBN 978-0-06-057939-5
(lib. bdg.)
[1. Camps—Fiction. 2. Family life—North Carolina—Fiction.
3. Creative ability—Fiction. 4. Eccentrics and eccentricities—
Fiction. 5. North Carolina—Fiction.] I. Title.
PZ7.T5735App 2012   2011019388
[Fic]—dc23   CIP
                                                        AC

Typography by Erin Fitzsimmons
12 13 14 15 16   CG/RRDH   10 9 8 7 6 5 4 3 2 1
❖
First Edition

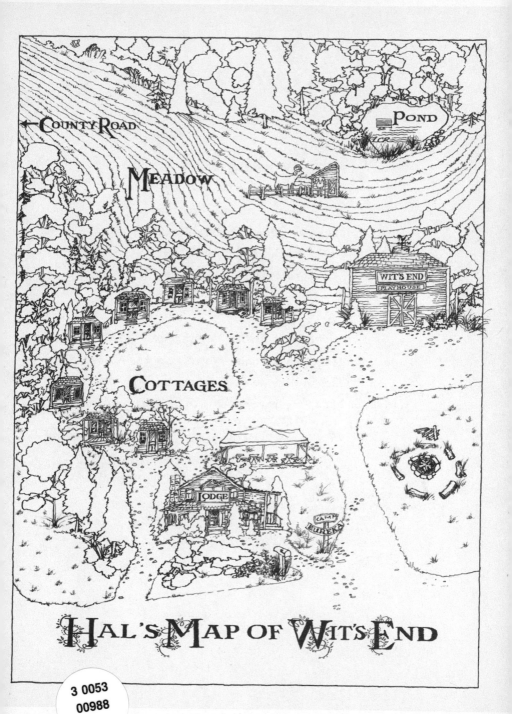

HAL'S MAP OF WIT'S END

Acknowledgments
Thanks to Larry Michael
of the North Carolina Department
of Environment and Natural Resources
for a delightful and very helpful
conversation concerning
camp regulations!

Thanks to Katherine Paterson
for coming up with the name Furniture of the Absurd
for Archie's work as we were writing the dramatic
adaptation of *Surviving the Applewhites.* Archie is grateful, too.

To all the Yunasa campers,
past, present, and future—
thanks for your inspiration!

P.S. Any resemblance to persons
living or dead is purely coincidental!

FAMILY
TREE

Sybil Jameson WIFE	**Randolph Applewhite** SON
Cordelia DAUGHTER	**Hal** SON
Edith (E.D.) DAUGHTER	**Destiny** SON

Zedediah
Applewhite
PATRIARCH

Archie
Applewhite
SON

Lucille
Applewhite
WIFE

Jake
Semple
BY INVITATION

The Cast of

APPLEWHITES AT WIT'S END

Permanent Residents of Wit's End

HUMAN

E.D. (Edith) Applewhite—
age thirteen, well organized and reliable
(the only noncreative member of the family),
third child of Randolph and Sybil

Randolph Applewhite—
professional theater director, husband of Sybil
and father of the four Applewhite children

Jake Semple—
age fourteen, the bad kid from the city,
the only non-Applewhite student at the family's
home school, the Creative Academy

Sybil Jameson—
author of the Petunia Grantham mystery novels, wife
of Randolph and mother of the Applewhite children

Destiny Applewhite—
age five, highly creative, extremely talkative,
youngest Applewhite child

Zedediah Applewhite—
patriarch of the Applewhite family, maker
of fine furniture, father of Randolph and Archie,
grandfather of the children

Archie Applewhite—
creator of Furniture of the Absurd, husband of
Lucille and uncle of the children

Lucille Applewhite—
poet, wife of Archie, aunt of the children,
sometime mystic and photographer

Cordelia Applewhite—
age seventeen, dancer-choreographer,
eldest Applewhite child

Hal Applewhite—
age sixteen, sculptor, painter, seriously
introverted second Applewhite child

OTHERS

Winston—
highly sensitive and slightly
overweight basset hound

Paulie—
Zedediah's adopted parrot, known for his
impressive vocabulary of curse words

Wolfbane (Wolfie)—
exceedingly bad-tempered male member
of Lucille's pair of rescue goats

Witch Hazel (Hazel)—
gentle and unassuming female goat

EUREKA! CAMPERS

Ginger Boniface—
age eleven, the green twin, poet

Cinnamon Boniface—
age eleven, the blue twin

Harley Schobert—
age twelve, son of indie rock stars, photographer

David Giacomo–
age fourteen, "angel" and Renaissance man

Quincy (Q) Brown–
age thirteen, dancer, singer, swimmer,
talent show winner

Samantha Peterman–
age twelve, passionate reader, visual artist

ASSORTED MINOR CHARACTERS
Bruno–
the Boniface chauffeur

Mrs. Montrose–
telephone voice, bane of Randolph's existence

Marlie Michaels–
Harley's considerably tattooed mother, lead singer of
Dragon's Blood

Mrs. Giacomo–
David's elegant mother

Mystery Driver of Plain Black Sedan

Daryl Gaffney–
telephone voice, assistant at the North Carolina
Department of Environment and Natural Resources

APPLEWHITES
AT WIT'S END

Chapter One

I t was a dark and stormy night when Randolph
Applewhite arrived home from New York to
announce the end of the world. The whole family
plus Jake Semple, the extra student at their home
school, the Creative Academy, were gathered at the
time around the fireplace in the living room of the
main house at Wit's End, while a wind howled and
snow swirled against the windows.

Like everyone else, E.D. had at first taken her father's
announcement to be hyperbole—one of her vocabulary
words for that week, which meant "deliberate and

obvious exaggeration for effect." A famous theater director, Randolph Applewhite had a habit of making exactly this announcement whenever something— almost anything—went wrong with a project of his and he felt the need for sympathy. So often had they heard it, in fact, that E.D.'s mother, the even more famous Sybil Jameson, author of the bestselling Petunia Grantham mystery novels, actually said, "That's nice, dear," as she struggled to pick up a stitch she had dropped in the scarf she was attempting to knit.

It wasn't until well into his explanation that she put down her needles and began paying attention. "What do you mean gone?"

"Just what I said! Gone! Embezzled!"

"How much of it?"

"All of it! To the last penny. The Applewhite family is destitute. We shall have to sell Wit's End and move to a hovel somewhere."

"What's a hovel?" asked E.D.'s five-year-old brother, Destiny, who was cheerfully and industriously drawing a bright spring-green pig on a large pad of newsprint.

When the whole story had at last been told—not until long after Destiny had been sent to bed and everyone else had finished a couple of mugs of hot cocoa enhanced with comforting marshmallows or alcohol, depending on their ages—it was clear that while the end of the Applewhites' world had not yet arrived, it was looming on the horizon like smoke from a wildfire and heading their way.

E.D. had never really understood—nor felt the need to—the financial structure that formed the foundation of her family's creative compound. She only knew that the whole, extended Applewhite family had left New York when Destiny was a year old and moved to rural North Carolina, where they had bought an abandoned motor lodge called the Bide-A-Wee. They had renamed it Wit's End and had lived here since, the adults following their particular creative passions and the children, except for E.D.'s own absolutely noncreative self, *discovering* theirs. All of the adults were famous. Her grandfather and her uncle Archie both designed and created furniture—Zedediah Applewhite's handcrafted wood furniture and Archie's "Furniture of the Absurd," which wasn't really so much furniture as sculpture and which was regularly exhibited in galleries around the country. Her aunt Lucille was a poet.

What E.D. learned that stormy winter night was that they had come to Wit's End not just so the family could live together, but so that they could pool their resources in order to continue their work. The vast majority of these resources came from the worldwide sales of the Petunia Grantham mysteries; some came from Zedediah's beautiful, expensive, and entirely practical furniture; and some came from Randolph's

3

work directing plays. Nothing else anyone did brought in much money. All of their resources had been gathered together in a family trust. The manager who had handled that trust, and therefore the future of the entire Applewhite enterprise, had turned out to be a crook.

"He'll go to jail," Randolph said after his second cup of bourbon-laced cocoa. "There's that, at least!"

"And what good will that do *us*?" Archie asked.

"I, for one, will feel better," Randolph answered. "It will cheer the dark nights in our hovel."

Zedediah, ever practical, pointed out that the Petunia Grantham mysteries would no doubt continue to sell as they always had, to which Sybil responded that she had only that morning killed Petunia Grantham off. The current novel, which was due to be finished within the week, would be the last in the series. "I killed her because I simply can't write another one. It would destroy my very soul."

"Your soul is tougher than that!" Randolph responded. "You can simply resurrect her in the next! They do it all the time in soap operas."

"My books are not soap operas!"

Only Aunt Lucille had taken the news of their sudden poverty in stride. She breathed a series of long, calming breaths, smiled, and announced that they would get along in some unforeseen way, just as they always had. All they needed to do was trust their creative energies, and they would surely come up with a way to solve the problem. "One step at a time," she said. "Out of the darkness, into the light."

"How long do we have?" Sybil asked then.

"If we gather up everything we have in the bank accounts, plus whatever you're owed when you turn in the current novel, plus the fees for the two directing gigs I have contracts for—assuming that Zedediah's furniture continues to sell the way it has—we can probably keep the mortgage paid through June. Maybe July. But after that . . ."

"We'll think of something," Lucille said. "Remember Shelley's 'Ode to the West Wind.' *'O Wind, / If Winter comes, can Spring be far behind?'*"

As it turned out, the winter was unusually harsh and unusually long, or at least it felt that way. By the time the Wit's End daffodils began blooming in March, the family had become obsessed with saving money in every way possible. The children's allowances had been not just cut, but actually discontinued. E.D.'s older brother, Hal, unable now to order sculpture supplies online for UPS delivery, had taken to going through the trash to find materials for his projects. "If it gets much worse," he complained, "I'll have to go back to painting! At least I have plenty of tubes of paint."

E.D.'s sister, Cordelia, had given up drinking her seaweed-and-protein health drinks. "I can't even afford the gas to get to the store, let alone the cost of the supplements! How am I going to maintain the energy to keep up my dancing?"

Winston, their food-loving basset hound, was now living on kibble instead of canned dog food, and liver treats had become a thing of the past. Zedediah's parrot, Paulie, could no longer count on fresh peanuts, and meat had become an occasional indulgence instead of the centerpiece of most dinners for the humans in the family. Pot roast, everybody's favorite dinner, had not been seen since the end of the world was announced. E.D. thought she had seen Uncle Archie at the goat pen from time to time, staring longingly at Wolfbane and Witch Hazel, Lucille's rescue goats.

E.D. herself had begun using the back sides of papers from the recycling box to write her research papers for school. And Zedediah had sped up production of his furniture, appearing in the kitchen late for dinner, still wearing his sawdust-covered work apron, and going right back to the woodshop afterward. So busy was he that Paulie had begun picking his feathers out from loneliness and perches had to be established for him throughout Wit's End. The last person to leave a room was supposed to take Paulie along so that he wouldn't be left by himself.

It was an evening in early March when Randolph, having just been paid by the theater in Raleigh where he'd directed a production of the musical *Oliver!* with

Jake, his newly discovered star, playing the role of the Artful Dodger, called a family meeting. He waved his check in the air. "This will cover another mortgage payment," he said. The Applewhites couldn't always be counted upon to celebrate one another's successes, but this time they broke into spontaneous cheers and applause. "Even better, I have a plan to save Wit's End!"

The cheers and applause died away. No one entirely trusted Randolph's ideas. "What is it?" E.D.'s mother asked suspiciously. She had steadfastly refused—citing the arrival of her Petunia Grantham royalty check as her fair contribution to the family bank account—to resurrect Petunia or begin another book, as she felt the need to rest her brain. "Your plans have been known to require considerable effort from the rest of us."

"All for one and one for all," Randolph said. "Just listen to me, everyone. You're going to love it!" He turned to Jake, who was sitting on the floor rubbing Winston's ears. "I owe a part of this idea to Jake. I was sitting in the theater, listening to him sing 'Consider Yourself at Home,' when it came to me. The next line of the song invites Oliver Twist into the family, just as we've invited Jake into ours. So there I was, looking at this stage full of singing and dancing kids—Fagin's pickpockets—and it occurred to me that we could create just such a family."

"A family of pickpockets?" Archie said. "I hardly

think that's the best way to solve our problem!"

"A family of creative kids! We invited Jake to join the Creative Academy. Why couldn't we take in a whole lot more? Not all year round—just in the summer. We'll start a camp for creative kids. I've even got a name for it. *Eureka!*" Randolph looked expectantly around the room. "Well? What do you think? People pay big money to send their kids to summer camp. Just regular summer camp. Think what they'd pay to have their kids spend eight weeks with a family of professional artists. *Famous professional artists*!"

"Kids? Living here with us?" Hal said, his face going pale. "How many?"

"I'm thinking just twelve this first year, a pilot group."

"And what would we do with these twelve kids?" Archie asked.

"Teach them. Encourage them. Share with them our love of art, our own individual creative passions. Set them on the path to becoming creative, productive adults! *Eureka!* would not only bring in big bucks, it would be a humanitarian endeavor—helping to groom the next generation of American artists. It will be a whole family project. There will be something for everyone to do."

"Me, too?" asked Destiny.

"Of course you, too. You can be the camp mascot!"

E.D. doubted that Destiny knew what a mascot

was, but the title was enough to satisfy him.

Randolph turned to his wife. "Now that Petunia Grantham's dead, you're going to need something to do! You can't rest your brain forever!"

"Twelve children? Twelve *other people's* children?"

"Yes. Think of it. Twelve delightful children into whose meager little lives we will bring the joys of art. We do art—and children—uncommonly well. Just look at our own four, and Jake, too, of course! Who would have thought when Jake first came to us that we could turn him into a musical-theater star in a matter of weeks? We could do that sort of thing with twelve more!"

E.D. suspected that Jake wasn't willing to give the Applewhite family *all* the credit for his newly discovered talent, but she could see that he was listening carefully as Randolph laid out the details of the camp. Each of them would share with the campers what they liked to do best, Randolph told them—their own creative passion—including Jake. As the only one besides Destiny able to sing at all, he could be the singing coach.

"And what would *I* share with them?" E.D. asked.

"A play needs a stage manager, a camp needs a—a— *an executive assistant*, the person who handles the schedule and the details and makes sure everything runs smoothly. You do that wonderfully well, E.D.— you know you do!"

No one but Destiny had yet accepted the idea. So Randolph went on, refusing to be daunted by their stony faces. "For heaven's sake, people. We're talking only eight weeks here! Practically no time at all. If we charge twelve families what I expect to charge them, we could save Wit's End, bring meat back to the family table, and restart allowances. Would you really rather sell out, leave here, and move to a hovel in Hoboken?"

Chapter Two

When Jake had first come to live at Wit's End, he had been determined to get away as soon as possible. Having been kicked out of the entire public school system of the state of Rhode Island, then out of Traybridge Middle School after he was sent to North Carolina to live with his grandfather, he had expected to get himself kicked out of the Applewhites' Creative Academy in a matter of days. The first problem with that had been that the Applewhites weren't the least bit bothered by his multiple piercings, his scarlet spiked hair, his black clothes, or his cursing—all the things that established his identity as the bad kid from the city. The second problem was that he really had no place else to go. His parents were both serving time in minimum-security prisons for having attempted to sell their home-grown marijuana to an off-duty sheriff's deputy, and there were no foster families back home in Providence willing to take him in. E.D. had almost gleefully pointed out that his only alternative was Juvie. So he'd been forced to stay.

It had turned out to be the best thing that ever happened to him. Becoming a musical-theater star in a matter of weeks had surprised Jake as much as it had surprised the Applewhites. He'd never suspected that he had a talent for singing and acting until Randolph recruited him to play Rolf in *The Sound of Music*. The show had been a success and Jake had gotten good reviews, but that hadn't been nearly as important as his discovery of what the Applewhites called a "creative passion." Never in his life had Jake been anywhere near as happy as he was onstage, in front of an audience, becoming a person quite different from himself. He loved singing. He loved acting. And later when Randolph cast him as the Artful Dodger in *Oliver!*, he'd found out that he loved dancing, too. Everything about musical theater, in fact, turned Jake on.

Because the Creative Academy was a home school,

he had been able to take off the whole month of February to be in *Oliver!*; and not only that, he'd been able to get school credit for doing it. He was theoretically in the seventh grade with E.D., but he didn't have to be stuck all the time doing what she did and being shown up by her obsessively organized, determinedly academic, and viciously competitive version of education. This was a girl who drove herself relentlessly toward perfection and couldn't bear the thought of getting (actually, thanks to the way the Applewhites did home schooling, *giving herself*) less than an A in anything. She and Jake might be very nearly the same age, but they were wildly and impossibly different. Thanks to the Applewhite philosophy of life, which passionately celebrated individuality, that was completely okay.

Randolph's end-of-the-world announcement had scared Jake clear down to his toes, though he'd done his best to hide it. What would suddenly poverty-stricken Applewhites do with *him*? He himself had no money. His grandfather was providing him with a small allowance so he could pay for clothes and a few incidentals, but otherwise he'd really been taken in as if he were a family member. He wasn't. He was another mouth to feed. Jake couldn't stand to lose his place here—it would mean losing himself. His new self. The only one he'd ever really known or cared about!

The morning after that dark and stormy night he'd worked up the nerve to ask Archie and Lucille—it was their Wisteria Cottage that he lived in—if they thought it was going to be possible for him to finish the school year.

"Don't be silly, Jake!" Lucille had proclaimed, "You're a full-time student. Of *course* you'll finish the year."

But as time went on and the austerity measures the Applewhites had adopted began to really pinch, Jake had started worrying about what would happen in the summer. Like regular schools, the Creative Academy's year ended in June. There'd be no reason to keep him here after that, so he figured they would probably send him to the grandfather he barely knew, a grandfather who had no clue about creative passion and who had only seen one musical in all his life: *The Sound of Music* last October at Wit's End Playhouse.

So when Randolph announced his idea for *Eureka!*, Jake had mostly held his breath until he heard the words he'd been hoping for: that he was to have a job to do at the camp. He didn't care that he didn't have the first clue about how to be a singing coach. He only cared that he wasn't going to be sent off to spend the summer alone on a ramshackle farm outside of Traybridge with his grandfather. Whatever camp turned out to be, it had to be better than that! He figured he was the happiest person in the room when the rest of the family had finally agreed to it.

Now, the very next night, the family was gathered for their first planning session. "What are we going to do with these kids all day?" Archie asked.

"Workshops, of course!" Randolph said. "Each of us, as I said in the first place, will share our own creative passion. We'll give them the whole spectrum of creative and artistic possibilities. I will do a theater workshop, of course, with an emphasis on acting."

"I can't teach twelve children how to make sculptural wood furniture in eight weeks," Archie protested.

"Well, then—how about Sculpture with Natural Materials?' Randolph said. "They can gather whatever they need from our own woods and meadows—thus saving a fortune on materials. You can certainly teach that."

Archie shook his head. "I don't want to teach! I want to do my own work."

Sybil quickly agreed.

"We're talking about saving our *lives* here!" Randolph reminded them. "There will still be plenty of time for each of you to do your own work. It isn't as if you'll have the campers the whole day!" Then he looked at Sybil. "You don't even *have* your own work, remember? A fiction workshop shouldn't be any problem at all. You *do* it so well, how hard could it be to teach?"

"I shall be in my element," Lucille said. "That poetry workshop I did at Traybridge Middle School

15

was a disappointment—one hour every other week. How can anyone instill a love for the sound and imagery and *soul* of poetry in five disconnected hours? Imagine having twelve young poets to mold and encourage on a daily basis for eight whole weeks, twelve young poets to introduce to the vast wealth of American contemporary poetry! I'll have them write every day, of course. We'll put out an anthology at the end of camp—or a journal of their work at the very least!"

"Children are not going to make fine wood furniture," Zedediah said.

"Of course not, Father! You can teach them the principles of design, the use of tools."

"No kids are going to get near my lathe—it would be a lawsuit waiting to happen."

"So have them make something simple. Wooden toys. Birdhouses. Focus on design. You know yourself that's the most creative part of what you do."

"I'll teach them ballet! Maybe a little modern dance," Cordelia said. "We can work up a presentation for the end of camp. Maybe a contemporary version of *Swan Lake* down by the pond."

Randolph turned to Hal. "With Archie doing sculpture, you can do a painting workshop. We've already got plenty of paint and brushes. And as short a time as you spent focused on painting, you must have a lot of canvas left over. We'll make Sweet Gum Cottage into an art studio."

"I can't do it," Hal said. "Twelve kids? No way!"

Jake tried to imagine Hal in Sweet Gum Cottage surrounded by twelve kids. He was such an introvert that Jake hadn't even laid eyes on him his first few weeks at Wit's End. When the whole family had decided to go on Facebook as an experiment in interacting with their fans, Hal had refused to friend anyone except himself.

E.D. spoke up then, counting off the workshops on her fingers. "Theater, dance, poetry, fiction, wood design, natural material sculpture, singing, and painting. If the workshops are an hour each—"

"Theater needs to be at least two hours. You can't get any momentum going in an hour!"

"So that's nine hours, not counting meals, rest periods, any kind of sports—"

"This is a creativity camp, not a sports camp!"

"Randolph," Lucille said, "these are children! They have to have physical activity of some kind."

"*Dance* is physical activity!" Cordelia said.

Lucille nodded. "True . . ." She thought for a moment and then smiled. "I can teach them yoga—perfect for balancing body, mind, and spirit. We'll start the day with it. Meditation first, then yoga—before breakfast."

"I've got the credentials to be a lifeguard," Archie said reluctantly. "I suppose we could offer swimming."

"*Gross!*" E.D. said. "Swimming in the pond? There are frogs and snakes and snapping turtles!"

"And muck," Jake added. Every time he and Winston went to the pond, the dog got covered with mud up to his stomach.

"Archie's right," Randolph said. "A camp should definitely have swimming. We can anchor a diving platform in the middle. The pond will make a wonderful picture for the brochure."

"Brochure!" Lucille said. "Yes, we have to let people know about us. We can replicate the advertising campaign we did for *The Sound of Music*. It worked splendidly!"

"Too expensive," Randolph said.

"Then we'll do most of it online," Archie said. "We'll need a *Eureka!* website."

"Somebody has to design a logo!"

E.D. was counting on her fingers again. "Swimming, yoga and meditation, meals, rest time, and all those workshops . . ."

"Campfires!" Sybil said. "Don't forget campfires. Toasting marshmallows—"

"S'mores!" Lucille added.

"Singing and storytelling," Sybil said. "We'll have to make a fire circle—over in the barn parking lot maybe."

"Don't forget free time," Zedediah said. "The creative spirit needs plenty of unscheduled time."

"There aren't enough hours in the day!" E.D. protested.

"Well then, they won't do everything every day," Randolph said. "You'll figure it out. You're a genius at calendars and scheduling."

Jake smiled to himself. His summer was secure. The Applewhites were off and running.

Chapter Three

With a jolt, E.D. realized she had fallen asleep over the computer keyboard. Again. She had been doing her online math course when the numbers had begun running together and she'd drifted off. Now she looked around at the ever-growing chaos of what had been the Creative Academy's schoolroom and sighed. Like just about everything at Wit's End, it was now partly what it had always been and partly something else. It was eleven o'clock in the morning on May seventh, almost exactly two months after Randolph had first brought up his plan, and she was the only one here, the only one still accomplishing anything that remotely resembled school. Jake was off in the woodshop with Archie building a diving platform for the pond. She had no idea what either Cordelia or Hal was up to, but she was certain it had to do with *Eureka!*

This was going to become the camp office, so the schoolroom's furniture and materials had been shoved to one side to make room for a somewhat dented metal desk, a threadbare swivel chair, and two enormous file cabinets that Archie had found at a used furniture store. Three of the school desks had already been carted off to the storage rooms in the bottom of the barn because nobody was using them. She was the only student at the Creative Academy who was determined to finish every single thing she had planned for spring semester. Everybody else had substituted camp preparations for most of their schoolwork. Math, which all of them took online, was the only part of regular school that went relentlessly on for Hal, Cordelia, and Jake, and all three of them complained bitterly about it. With final exams approaching, they were pretty much forced to keep up.

E.D. absolutely refused to let *Eureka!* derail her. Since that first planning meeting, she had finished three research papers (for science, history, and current events), read four books and written book reports (for language arts), kept up her vocabulary study, and maintained a steady A average in math. If camp was supposed to save their way of life, she didn't see how it could do that by destroying hers! So even though she'd been up late the night before creating the fifth— *fifth!*—version of a weekly schedule that could include all the camp activities everyone thought were absolutely necessary, she was still managing to stay on her own daily school schedule—except for occasional accidental catnaps.

She swiveled her chair around to look at the list she'd posted on the wall by the door. It was a list of all the things that needed to be done to make the camp happen, and it stretched from very near the ceiling all the way down to the floor. Everyone in the family had contributed to the list, including Destiny, who wanted them to build tree houses for the campers to live in, to bury play money all over Wit's End, and then to make pirate costumes for treasure hunting. Those, at least, didn't actually have to be done. Her father had added an enormous number of *absolutely necessary tasks* and then headed cheerfully off to Pennsylvania to direct another play. "Just like you," her mother had complained to him, "leaving the rest of us to do all the work!"

"*All* the work? Don't be ridiculous," he'd said as he stowed his suitcases in the trunk of his Miata. "I'll be back in plenty of time to help with the most difficult job of all: winnowing the hundreds of applications we get to find the best possible candidates, the cream of the creative crop. Everything that needs to be done between now and then will be an exhilarating challenge for the whole family! Don't think of it as work; think of it as stretching boundaries, galvanizing energies. Meanwhile, I'll be all by myself in Pennsylvania, slaving away in the theatrical salt mines to keep the mortgage paid."

E.D. had thought about her father's words quite a lot in the weeks after he'd left. It had been a challenge, all right. By now a lot of entries on the to-do list had been crossed out, but there were still an unsettling number to go. Hal had designed the camp logo, and Uncle Archie had built the website. Randolph had *driven* to his directing gig in Philadelphia instead of flying, as he normally would have, so they could use the money he'd saved on airfare to finance the advertising campaign.

There hadn't yet been leaves on the trees when the brochure and website deadline had arrived, so Lucille couldn't take any new pictures. She'd gathered photographs of Wit's End from family albums and then spent days on end Photoshopping in images of happy campers she'd found on the internet so they appeared to be frolicking in what the brochure called "the summer glory of *Eureka!*'s natural setting."

Then there had been the problem of creating the camp application. "It needs to give us a sure way to determine who belongs to that 'cream of the crop' Randolph wants and who doesn't," Sybil pointed out. "We'll need a form for basic information, and lots of supporting materials, too—like samples of the children's creative work."

"We should require recommendations from teachers and coaches . . . ," E.D. had added.

"And an essay from the child explaining why he or she wants to attend," Lucille added. "I want to see something of their thought process."

"Not everybody likes to write," Archie had protested. "We need to let them send a video instead—let them talk if they want."

There had been several major arguments and three revisions before Zedediah was able to put the forms and instructions up on the website and cross "application" off the list.

When the advertising budget ran out, Sybil managed to get free publicity with some small stories printed in various newspapers around the country and on a great many parenting blogs. Apparently there were millions of parents across the country who believed they were raising creative geniuses, because the news of *Eureka!* quickly went viral. The *Eureka!* website's e-mail account was deluged with inquiries from parents. The trouble was that almost all of them asked for—or demanded—scholarships for their prodigiously talented children. "I don't understand it!" Sybil moaned. "We don't mention *scholarships* anywhere!"

"Yes, but we did mention the fees," Archie said. "Astronomical fees!"

"Tell them the *Eureka!* scholarship fund has already been exhausted," Zedediah said dryly. "Like the advertising budget."

As the application deadline approached, Lucille, who'd been put in charge of collecting the applications, reported that two had arrived, then a third. "Three? Three total?" Sybil said. "From all those thousands of inquiries? This is a disaster!"

Aunt Lucille dismissed Sybil's concerns. "You know how creative people are. They put things off till the last minute. We'll get an avalanche of applications the week after the deadline."

E.D. turned back to her math now. It was the last schoolwork she was likely to get done today. Her father had arrived home last night, grumpy from the long drive. He had dragged his suitcases in from the car, kissed her mother, and gone straight up to bed, saying he couldn't possibly deal with anything *Eureka!* until he'd had a good, long sleep. The meeting to catch him up on their progress and begin winnowing applications was scheduled for this afternoon.

⌘

"Seven? What do you mean *seven*?" Randolph roared when Lucille set the basket of applications on the table where the family had just finished lunch.

"Seven, seven, seven!" Paulie repeated quietly from his perch in the corner.

"She means that we have received a total of seven applications," Zedediah said. "Period."

Lucille nodded. "Think of it this way. At least we don't have to spend the whole afternoon winnowing."

There was a considerable period of silence.

E.D. thought of all the effort that had gone into creating the application. They could have just asked for names and addresses and been done with it.

"We'll just have to accept all of them then," Randolph said. "We needed twelve campers to pay the mortgage off entirely, but I think we can survive with seven. *Barely*."

There was another silence. "What?" he said. "Why is everybody looking at me?"

"I'm not looking at you, Daddy!" Destiny said from his stool at the end of the table. "I'm drawing Pooh and Piglet in the woods!" Destiny had recently become entirely obsessed with drawing.

"You might want to look at that first application on the top of the pile," Sybil said.

Randolph picked up the sheaf of paper-clipped pages and scanned the top sheet. "Priscilla Montrose? *That* Priscilla Montrose?"

"You think there's another in Traybridge?" Archie said.

"Oh, no. No, no, no! Absolutely not! We are not having that child at our camp."

E.D. sighed. It was Randolph's utter refusal to cast Priscilla Montrose in *The Sound of Music* last fall that had led Priscilla's mother, the president of the board of the Traybridge Little Theatre, to cancel the production he had been hired to direct. That had led the Applewhites to turn their barn into a theater and create the Wit's End Playhouse so the show could go on. As successful as that show had been, Randolph had not forgiven Mrs. Montrose for canceling it in the first place.

"That child has less talent than a sea slug!" he said now. "She not only isn't the cream, she isn't even the *skim milk* of the creative crop! I will not have Priscilla Montrose at *Eureka!* under any circumstances whatsoever."

"Maybe you should consider that this is a child who really *needs* us!" Lucille offered.

"And it could certainly be argued that we need her," Zedediah added.

"Clearly," Archie said, "we can't afford to be choosy."

Randolph looked at the application again. Then he leafed through the pages. "We couldn't take her anyway," he said. "Not from this application. Look at this signature!" He pointed to the line where the parent was supposed to sign the form. "Priscilla has quite obviously forged her mother's signature."

"Think of it as a sign of independence!" Sybil said.

"This is not a valid application. The child has gone behind her mother's back. I'll make you a bet she was *forbidden* to apply. That hateful, spiteful, vengeful woman would never allow her child to spend the summer with us!"

"I was afraid you'd take this stand," said Sybil with a sigh.

"We can survive with six campers," Randolph said. "We'll just have to cut a few corners, that's all. Be a little more frugal."

E.D. shook her head. *Frugal* had been another of her vocabulary words: "characterized by thriftiness and avoidance of waste," it meant. They'd had peanut butter and jelly sandwiches for lunch—for the third time that week. She didn't think they could be any more frugal than they already were.

Chapter Four

Once it was clear there was no application winnowing to be done, Archie left the meeting to go pick up the swimming pool ladder he had bought from Craigslist for the diving platform. He took Destiny with him and told Jake he'd need some help when they got back. Meantime, Jake was eager to hear who the campers were that he was going to have in his singing workshop.

Lucille and Sybil had spent a long time going over the applications and were now taking turns presenting the campers to the family. It occurred to Jake halfway through Lucille's presentation of the first one—a thirteen-year-old boy named Quincy Brown—that he hadn't really thought this whole camp idea through. There had been some vague image in his mind of a bunch of little kids he could get singing with him, the way he'd done with Destiny. *Little kids.* Not somebody almost his own age who had won so many talent shows that he was paying for camp himself from his winnings!

When Sybil began talking about the next two—a pair of eleven-year-old twins named Ginger and Cinnamon Boniface—Hal began to hyperventilate. He excused himself and went up to his room. "He'll get used to the idea by the time they come," Lucille assured everyone. "It's only six kids."

After Sybil and Lucille finished talking about all of them—three girls and three boys—Jake felt a headache coming on. He'd taken a few notes so he could fill Archie in, but E.D. was going to make up a booklet of camper bios so everybody could have a copy. "It's important for all of you to *memorize* the bios," she said in her usual bossy way, "so you'll be ready to handle the campers."

Jake didn't see how memorizing all the great accomplishments these kids had put on their applications would help him get ready to handle anybody.

"One of them is the son of rock stars!" he told Archie later as he held the ladder Archie was attaching to the diving platform.

Destiny was sitting on the floor pounding nails into a board Archie had given him. "Rock stars?" he asked. "You mean those guys E.D. has pitchers of on her ceiling?"

"Not those rock stars," Jake said. "The kid's parents have an indie rock band called Dragon's Blood."

"They have a cult following among high school and college kids," Archie said.

"Yeah. His mom's the lead singer; his dad is lead guitar."

Destiny stopped pounding. "He gots a guitar for a dad?"

"His dad *plays* the guitar. The kid's name is Harley—he was named for his father's motorcycle."

Archie groaned.

"His mother wrote a note on his application that she hopes the camp will give him a new outlet for his creative abilities. Right now he's into photography, but he only takes pictures of dead things."

"Eeeww," Destiny said. "Where's he get dead things?"

"She didn't say. Then there's Quincy Brown," Jake said, "who calls himself Q. He's thirteen and the only African American. He's won something like ten talent shows. He sings. He dances. And he's been in more musicals than I have."

"Feeling a little intimidated, are you?" Archie asked.

"A little?" Jake said. "Besides those two there's David. He's *fourteen*! My age. He's had professional coaches—singing, dancing, *and* acting coaches—since he was three! Plus, he wrote a play that was done at his private school in Virginia last semester—with him in the lead. According to his mother, David is a *genius*: God's gift to all things creative."

Archie finished screwing in the ladder. "That's his mother talking. Remember Mrs. Montrose. Don't believe what a mother says about her talented kid. Not till you meet him and see his work."

"Okay, but how am I going to be singing coach for dudes my age who've had more experience than I've had and real, professional coaching? What makes me any different from the campers?"

Archie laughed. "What makes you different? You're you and they're them! Think about what my dear wife says about you, Jake: you are a *radiant light being*. Lucille is never wrong."

Jake frowned. "Yeah, but she'd say that about the campers too. She thinks that about everyone."

"Am I a light being?" asked Destiny.

"You're practically blinding!" Archie told him. "So, Jake. There are plenty of ways to show your individuality. Why did you get all those piercings and dye your hair red and spike it all over your head? So you'd stand out, right? So you'd scare off the people you didn't want to deal with!"

"I don't know. I guess. Is that why you got your tattoos?"

Archie looked down at the anchor on one forearm and the dragon on the other, and laughed. "Just the opposite. When I decided I wanted to work my way around the world on a tramp steamer, I was a skinny high school dropout with a ponytail who wore Birkenstocks and tie-dyed T-shirts. I wasn't sure I could even get a shipboard job, but if I did, I figured the rest of the crew would give me no end of trouble. So I worked out for a couple of months to build up some muscle, got myself a crew cut, and then went to a tattoo parlor down by the docks. I had the guy there give me his two most popular designs."

"And it worked?"

"Yep. By the time I got back to New York a couple of years later, the look had come to feel like me. So I've kept it ever since. Funny thing is that it was like *camouflage* on the ship—I blended into the background. But now it pretty much guarantees I'll stand out in an art gallery. It's not just the look that counts; it's the context. If you want to separate yourself from the campers, you could just go back to your old look."

Jake shrugged. "The hair was a pain to keep up—the dye and the gel and all."

Archie looked at Jake's dark brown hair—nicely grown out from the buzz cut he'd had in the fall for *The Sound of Music*. "You know Lucille cuts my hair—she's a whiz with the clippers. She could give you a Mohawk. You wouldn't have to do much with it—maybe a little wax—and I guarantee that, with all your piercings and a Mohawk, you'll at least *look* plenty different from the campers."

"What's a Mohawk?" Destiny asked. "Can I have one too? Does it gots colors?"

"No colors," Jake said.

"And no Mohawk for you," Archie added. "Would you please go find Hal and ask him to help us get the platform anchored in the pond?"

Destiny put down his hammer and folded his arms across his chest, his lower lip sticking out. "Not unless I gets to have a Mohawk like Jake."

"Tell you what," Archie said. "If your mother says yes, Lucille will cut your hair too."

"Yay, I'm gonna gets a Mohawk!" Destiny said, and ran out of the woodshop.

Jake and Archie went out on the porch to wait for Hal. "The thing is," Jake said, "not looking like the other campers doesn't mean I can be their singing coach!"

"You have an advantage over them. You've seen

their applications and know what they've done. In the camp publicity you're billed as a prodigy, and that's all they'll know. If you act like you know what you're doing, they'll just assume you do. So tell me about the girls."

"A pair of eleven-year-old identical twins—one's a poet."

"Lucille must be thrilled. What about the other one?"

Jake thought for a moment and then shrugged. "I don't remember. The third girl—Samantha—is into visual arts. The portfolio she sent looks like a set of illustrations for a fantasy novel. Lots of elves in the woods."

"It promises to be an interesting eight weeks," Archie said.

"Yeah, *interesting.*"

Chapter Five

It was June 27. The first day of camp. E.D. swiveled the desk chair and looked around what had been the schoolroom. Nothing was left of the Creative Academy except the clock on the wall, now reading 10:14, and the old computer table made of a door resting on a pair of filing cabinets. The computer and printer were still there, but instead of random piles of books and papers, the door now held a used copier and a laundry basket containing brightly colored plastic water bottles from the dollarstore in Traybridge. Her father had decreed that every camper needed to have a water bottle at all times in case of dehydration or heat prostration. They'd bought extras on the grounds that creative kids were scattered and forgetful and would probably lose them frequently. There was a stack of canvas bags on which Cordelia had painted the *Eureka!* logo, because Lucille had decided that all of the campers needed some way of carrying a notebook, pens, and whatever else they might need as they moved from workshop to workshop during the camp day. Bags, notebooks, and pens had also been purchased from the dollarstore.

A counter made of scrap lumber and painted somewhat randomly in Destiny's favorite primary colors (by Destiny) now stretched across most of the room a few feet inside the door. On that counter were a sign saying CAMP OFFICE and a vase of silk flowers. The used office furniture was arranged in the space behind the counter, and the dented desk at which E.D. was sitting now held a new and complicated-looking telephone as well as the first-week schedules she had been stapling together for the campers. A large and rather fanciful map of Wit's End that Hal had drawn covered much of one wall, and the rest was taken up with a densely filled-in calendar with today's date circled in red, plus copies of all the materials that had been sent to the campers' families and the schedule for the day. The original to-do list had been taken down, even though several entries hadn't yet been crossed off.

Between two and five this afternoon, the campers would arrive and *Eureka!* would start, whether they were ready or not. And of course, E.D. thought, they were not! The dining tent, rented from a discount wedding supply house, was supposed to have been delivered two days ago but hadn't come till this morning. Uncle Archie was out behind the house with Jake now putting it up. He should have been in the woodshop instead, helping to finish the dock Zedediah had designed for the pond to keep campers from having to tromp through the muck to get into the water.

Jake appeared in the doorway, his dark brown Mohawk standing up down the center of his otherwise newly shaved head. His eyebrow ring and all of his earrings were in place, and he was gleaming with sweat. He held out a stack of army surplus blankets. "Your mother wants these on the beds. Do you have a few minutes to help me?"

"What're you doing here?" E.D. asked him. "You're supposed to be helping Uncle Archie put up the dining tent!"

"It's up. Archie's gone back to helping your grandfather with the dock." He wiped the sweat from his face on the sleeve of the official *Eureka!* staff T-shirt Lucille had designed. "I don't know why Sybil thinks the campers are going to need blankets. It's freaking hot out there already."

The phone rang. E.D. picked it up. "Good morning,

38

you've reached *Eureka!*, the unparalleled summer experience for creative kids."

She listened for a moment, put her hand over the mouthpiece, and groaned. Why hadn't she checked caller ID? The grating, heavily North Carolina-accented voice was unmistakable. "It's Mrs. Montrose," she mouthed silently to Jake as she punched the phone's speaker button.

The woman's voice filled the room. "I demand to speak to Randolph Applewhite! Who is this?"

Jake set the blankets on the counter.

"This is E.D. Applewhite, Mrs. Montrose," she said, her voice as neutral as she could make it. "I'm afraid my father is not here at the moment." Her father and Destiny had left fifteen minutes earlier for the airport in Greensboro to pick up the two campers who were coming as unaccompanied minors. She would have had to lie otherwise, of course. This was not a day for Randolph Applewhite to talk to Mrs. Montrose. "How may I help you?"

"You tell your father, young lady, that I would never have allowed my daughter to apply to his so-called creativity camp if I had known she was doing it. As far as I'm concerned, the man has not the slightest understanding of the sensitive psyche of a highly creative child—"

E.D. shook her head. Highly creative children were the *only* ones her father understood.

"There should be some sort of law to keep that man

from interacting with anyone under the age of thirty," the irritating voice went on. "My daughter went behind my back to fill out the forms and gather the required teacher recommendations. She submitted that application entirely on her own. But once she did so, proving to me how strong is her wish to make a career in the arts, I was naturally compelled to support her. Your father had the audacity to *reject her application*! My daughter's self-esteem has been irreparably damaged by his callous disregard for her talent and potential."

E.D. rolled her eyes at Jake.

"Refusing to cast her in *The Sound of Music* last autumn was inexcusable," the woman continued. "But rejecting her camp application was an act of pure vindictiveness. I am quite certain he only did it to get back at me. Her talent is unquestionable. I recently sent him letters from experts in three—*three*—separate fields of creative endeavor recommending that he reverse his decision and accept my daughter. If *any* child belongs at a camp for highly creative children, my Priscilla does! But he has refused."

E.D. hadn't heard about any expert recommendations. Probably her father had simply thrown them away.

"I hold your father solely responsible for the fact that Priscilla has been crying herself to sleep every night. She's devastated! She had been absolutely counting on a summer of companionship with other creatively gifted children. *You tell him he has not heard the last of this.*"

"I'm terribly sorry for Priscilla's distress, and I'm certain my father is as well." E.D. took a breath and then went on. "But really, there was nothing we could do. By the time those expert recommendations were received, the camp was completely filled up. All the places were taken within a week of the application deadline."

Jake began to laugh and hurriedly put a hand over his mouth.

"Thank you for calling, Mrs. Montrose," E.D. said. "I'll be sure to give my father your message." She hung up. "Thank goodness we didn't take her kid. Imagine that woman hovering over us all summer. Listen, I don't have time to help with the blankets. Just put them on the ends of the bunks! I bet the campers won't use them a single time all summer."

After the success of *The Sound of Music* last fall, the family had decided to air-condition Wit's End. But they had only finished the main house, Zedediah's and Archie and Lucille's cottages, the woodshop, and the dance studio before the end of the world. The campers were going to have to depend on North Carolina breezes to cool their cottages. "Roughing it" is what Randolph called it.

"At least your new haircut ought to be cool," E.D. said.

Jake ran a hand through his hair and grinned. "Cool and easy. Destiny's having fits because your mother won't let him get a Mohawk too."

E.D. sighed. Jake was an appalling role model. She had been hoping to help her little brother avoid the curse of the creative flake by instilling in him habits of organization and good sense while he was still young enough for them to stick, but the moment Jake came into their lives that hope had turned to dust. She divided her life now into BJ and AJ: Before Jake and After Jake. Until he came, E.D. had thought there were basically two kinds of people in the world: chaotic creatives like everybody else in her family, and normal, stable, sensible people like herself. Jake didn't fit into either camp. He had both an Applewhite-esque creative streak and a genuine ability for organization and follow through. Unfortunately, it wasn't the organization and follow-through side of him that appealed to Destiny.

Just then Winston began his hysterical "terrorists coming, terrorists coming" combination of howling and barking outside. Most of Winston's terrorist alarms were figments of his imagination caused by the occasional vehicle that happened to pass Wit's End on the road out beyond the driveway. But this time the alarm was followed immediately by the sound of a car on the gravel driveway.

"Who could it be?" E.D. looked at the clock: 10:27.

"It's way, *way* too early to be a camper!"

By the time E.D. and Jake got out onto the front porch, the driver of the shiny black Mercedes with heavily tinted windows that was parked in front of the main house was leaning on the horn. The sound was driving the dog into ever more frenzied howling, though by now he was backing slowly but purposefully toward the porch, the fur on his neck and back standing straight up.

"Inside, Winston," E.D. said, holding the screen door open.

The frantic dog turned, nearly tripping over his ears, and scuttled safely into the house, where he continued to bark menacingly.

The horn went still. For a moment nothing happened. The car windows were so dark it was impossible to tell who might be inside.

Aunt Lucille appeared at the door now, her cascades of blond curls coming loose from the flowered scarf she had wrapped around her head, her hands covered with flour. She pushed Winston out of the way with one foot and came out onto the porch, brushing the flour from her hands, just as the back window of the Mercedes went slowly down and two identical faces peered out. "This had better be *Eureka!*" one of the faces said. "We've been driving in circles for an hour!"

Chapter Six

The driver's side door of the Mercedes opened. "Of course it's *Eureka!*" a gruff voice bellowed. "Didn't you see the sign?"

A man wearing a chauffeur's cap above a New York Yankees T-shirt, tattered blue jeans, and sandals got out of the car, stretching his legs and groaning. Ignoring Lucille, Jake, and E.D., he came around and opened the back door so the identical bodies that went with the identical faces could get out.

Cinnamon and Ginger Boniface. The twins from

New Jersey. The twins were eleven years old, Jake knew, but in person they didn't look it. As thin and small as they were, they could have passed for third graders. Both had short, curly, carrot-orange hair and pale skin sprinkled with freckles. They wore matching shorts and beaded tank tops—one green, one blue—matching sequined flip-flops, and long, sparkly earrings. Their finger- and toenails were painted the color of their clothes. They stood in the gravel drive now, frowning identical frowns.

Lucille was hurrying down the steps to greet them, still brushing flour from her hands. "Welcome, welcome, welcome, girls!" she said as she went. "Welcome to *Eureka!* I'm Lucille Applewhite." She held out her hand to the nearest twin, but the girl kept hers at her side.

"The poet!" the other twin said, her frown vanishing. "I'm a poet, too."

"Of course you are," Lucille said. "You won an award!" She used her still-outstretched hand to point first to E.D. and then to Jake. "This is E.D. Applewhite and that's Jake Semple."

In spite of his fresh Mohawk, the twins barely glanced at Jake. He could feel his jaw clenching. He'd expected, at least, to be noticed.

The man nodded at the green twin, "Ginger," and then at the blue, "Cinnamon."

"Well, girls, you're a little early, I'm afraid," Lucille

said. "The other campers won't be here till—"

"Between two and five P.M., *like the schedule says*," E.D. said with a familiar edge to her voice. She had sent the opening-day schedule electronically, Jake knew, as well as including it in the precamp packet she had sent to every family by snail mail.

"We're really, really glad to have you, though!" Lucille put in quickly. She turned to the man, who had popped the trunk and was hurriedly dragging out blue and green suitcases and duffel bags.

"Are you—are you Mr. Boniface?"

"Nope. Name's Bruno. Theodore Boniface's driver."

"I see. We were under the impression you'd be doing the whole trip today. We weren't expecting the girls to get here till around five."

"Somethin' came up, and Mr. Boniface needs me back tonight. We came as far as a hotel in Raleigh last night."

"*Motel*," the blue twin said. "That didn't even have a pool!"

"I should'a been on the road an hour ago. Stupid GPS didn't work for—"

"I'm so sorry you got lost," Lucille interrupted. "We sent directions—didn't we, E.D.?"

"You should have received them with *the schedule*," E.D. said to the man.

He hefted a blue-and-green plaid steamer trunk from the car and dumped it on the drive with the other luggage. "I hope somebody can get this stuff where it belongs. I gotta be starting back right now."

The twin in blue squinted up into the sun. "Is it always this hot here? Where's the pool? There's supposed to be a pool!"

"A pond, actually," Lucille said. "It's quite lovely. Entirely natural."

"There's a tour of the grounds scheduled for *after the other campers arrive*," E.D. told her.

"Does that dog bite?" the green twin asked. Winston's barking had subsided, replaced by the occasional *whuff* to show he was still keeping an eye on things. "I'm not staying if he bites."

Jake shook his head. "He's just nervous."

Jake had intended to lock Winston in Wisteria Cottage while the campers were arriving. The dog was frightened of new people till he got to know them. There was no way Jake could have known he should do it this early.

Lucille was holding on to her welcoming smile, but Jake could tell it was taking an effort. "Jake," she said, "why don't you take those duffel bags down to Dogwood Cottage for the girls."

Jake went down the porch steps as the driver pulled a pair of tennis rackets from the trunk. "Might as well take those back with you," Jake said. "No tennis court here."

"No tennis court!" the blue twin wailed.

47

Bruno put the rackets back and closed the trunk. "Nice to meet you," he said to Lucille. "Good luck!" He got back into the car. "See you in August," he called to the girls. He slammed the door and started the car.

"See you," the green twin said.

"Whatever," said the other.

As Jake went to pick up a duffel bag, the Mercedes roared away, spitting gravel. He could understand the man's hurry to get away from the twins even if he didn't have to be back in New Jersey that night.

"No tennis court!" the blue twin said again. "What kind of a camp is this anyway?"

Jake had already thrown the first duffel bag over his shoulder, picked up the other one, and started down the path that led to the cottages.

Chapter Seven

E.D. heard Aunt Lucille take a *deep, calming breath*. "You go on back to the kitchen," E.D. told her. "I'll help these two settle in. Get your suitcases, girls. I'll take you to your bunk." Mercedes and a driver or not, there was no reason these two couldn't get their own bags to their bunk.

The screen closed behind Aunt Lucille. The twins had made no move toward their suitcases. The green twin was staring up into the trees next to the house, an abstracted look on her face. With disapproving eyes, the blue twin, hands on her hips, scanned the house, then the yard, and finally what could be seen of the barn above the bushes. E.D. went down the stairs and found herself seeing Wit's End suddenly—really seeing it—as the campers would.

Some shingles were missing from the porch roof, and the main house badly needed a paint job. It was a stark contrast with the bright new sign Archie had made proclaiming it to be the Lodge. They couldn't have afforded to paint the house; but why had no one thought, when the sign was hung, to clean the heavy, gray tangles of spiderwebs from around the eaves or to scrub the green algae or mold or whatever it was creeping up the siding from the ground?

The scraggly combination of grass and various North Carolina weeds that constituted the front lawn had grown tall enough to be putting out seeds and a few raggedy flowers. And the barn, in spite of all the work that had been done last year to turn it into a theater, still looked shabby from the outside. There, too, the sign over the double doors, with its gold leaf lettering—WIT'S END PLAYHOUSE—made the dull, flaking, barn red paint look even worse by comparison.

E.D. started down the gravel path toward the cottages. "The girls' cottage is called Dogwood," she said, acutely aware of how much less picturesque it was than its name. All of the cottages at Wit's End, built in the 1940s when it had been turned from a failing farm into a motor lodge, had been white originally but over the years had weathered to a silvery gray. Their roofs were thick with moss. The southern mixed-deciduous forest—sweet gums, beeches, hickory, and oak trees, with a few tall pines—might seem to be closing in on them. Her mother liked to say the cottages blended perfectly into their surroundings. Someone else might say their surroundings were gobbling them up.

E.D. spoke as cheerfully as she could, considering how angry she was that the girls had arrived so early. It wasn't their fault, she reminded herself. "Just grab your suitcases and come along. I'll take you there."

"What about our trunk?" the blue twin asked. Her voice, E.D. thought, was an irritating whine.

"Jake'll be back to get it any minute." She continued down the path, assuming the girls would come after her. Behind her she heard a loud, theatrical sigh. Then there was the sound of scraping gravel, followed by a series of bumps and thumps and curses. She turned back. The wheels on the two suitcases had dug trenches in the path and were now jammed against little piles of gravel. The twins were standing there, looking helpless.

"They won't go any farther," the green twin said.

"Well then," E.D. said, determinedly hanging on to cheerfulness, "I guess you'll just have to *pick them up!*" She turned back toward Dogwood Cottage.

Green twin Ginger, blue twin Cinnamon, she repeated in her head as she walked. She would take them to their cottage, but that was absolutely all she would do with them. She wasn't their counselor; Cordelia was. She would leave them at Dogwood and go find Cordelia. It wasn't her fault they had come nearly four hours early. What kind of parents spent a fortune to send their kids to camp and then totally ignored that camp's very clear instructions about when to get them there? For that matter, what kind of parents sent two eleven-year-olds halfway across the country accompanied only by a surly chauffeur? *Green twin Ginger, blue twin Cinnamon.*

Behind her the twins were complaining to each other now about the heat and humidity and how heavy their suitcases were. "Where do you suppose Maria packed our swimming suits?" one of them asked the other. "I gotta get in the water."

E.D. wondered who Maria might be. A maid, maybe. *Maid. Chauffeur. Mercedes.* These were not kids who would take well to roughing it. When the cottage came into sight, Jake was nowhere to be seen. He had left the duffel bags on the porch and disappeared. Just like him to go off and leave everything to her.

E.D. went up onto the slightly sagging porch, stepped over the duffel bags, and held the screen door open for the twins. They bounced their suitcases up the stairs and around the duffel bags, and dragged them inside.

Cinnamon immediately left hers in the middle of the living room and began inspecting the walls, lifting pictures to peer behind them and feeling behind bookcases. "Where's the thermostat? Somebody needs to turn up the air-conditioning. It's an oven in here!"

"No thermostat. No air-conditioning." E.D. pointed to the open windows. "The bunks are cooled by outside air."

"Cooled? Cooled? You have got to be kidding! People could die of heat like this."

E.D. knew this wasn't true. She had lived at Wit's End without air-conditioning for four whole summers. "It'll be better at night." This wasn't entirely true, either, of course.

"That's it! I'm out of here." A phone seemed to have materialized in Cinnamon's hand. She was biting her lip and pressing on the screen. "Dad will just have to send Bruno back for us."

Would that mean refunding the twins' deposit? E.D. wondered.

Ginger had gone off down the hall to explore the bedrooms. "Hey, the back bedroom isn't too bad," she called. "It's all shaded by trees." There was a brief pause. "And there's a breath of a breeze. Oh! Listen! Did you hear that? Shaded by trees—breath of a breeze. It's the start of a poem!"

"You two can have that room if you want," E.D. told Cinnamon.

Cinnamon swore and peered at her phone. "What's the matter? I'm not getting a ring."

"You probably don't get service here," E.D. said. "There's only one tower."

"Look at this," Cinnamon said, holding her phone out to no one in particular. "No bars! Not one single bar! I've never seen that before."

"That's because you live in New Jersey," E.D. said. "This is North Carolina. The *country*. If your phone doesn't match our one tower, you don't have service. Period. Anyway, we sent you the list of rules. Rule three: no cell phones."

"Mother said that had to mean no cell phones *during sessions*. You know, like no cell phones in class at school. You can't expect us not to have a phone! What if there's an emergency?"

"*Our* cells work here. Plus, there are land lines. This is the country, not a desert island. Count yourself lucky—since your phone doesn't work, we won't have to confiscate it!"

"Cinn, come on back here," Ginger called from the bedroom. "There's a real, live hummingbird out there by some big orange flower. Come look!"

Cinnamon swore again and put her phone in the pocket of her shorts. "First chance I get, I'm calling Dad. We're going home." She raised her voice then. "Did you hear that, Ginger? *We're going home!*" But she went down the hall.

"The bathroom's on the right," E.D. called after her. "I'll go get your counselor."

Chapter Eight

Jake had dropped the duffel bags at the girls' cottage and was on his way to the woodshop to help Archie and Zedediah with the floating dock, kicking gravel as he walked. His grandfather had told him, the day he'd dropped Jake off at Wit's End to join the Creative Academy, "Those who sow the wind will reap the whirlwind." His grandfather had been making some sort of point about the behavior that had gotten Jake in trouble, but now Jake had a niggling suspicion that starting a camp was sowing the wind, and the Boniface twins were the first signs of the approaching whirlwind.

Before the day was out there would be four more kids besides the twins. He waved a hand in front of his eyes to shoo away a cluster of gnats. That's pretty much what he'd done with people all his life, he thought. He'd shooed them away—turned them off, scared them. He hadn't really known how to do anything else. There were some guys back at school in Rhode Island who he used to hang out with, guys who were as intimidating as he was. Kids and teachers all pretty much did their best to avoid them, which was what they wanted. The thing was, he hadn't really known those guys. They were all too busy showing how tough and cool they were to find out what any of them were like behind the image.

Now that he had the new haircut that was supposed to make him stand out from the other campers, he wondered if that was really what he wanted. Part of what he'd loved about being in the shows Randolph had cast him in was hanging out with other kids who liked what they were doing as much as he did. Like Jeannie Ng, who had played Liesl and given him his first stage kiss—his first kiss of any kind, though he hadn't admitted that to anybody. There'd been her brother, too, and most of the guys from *Oliver!* They'd all become his friends. The first friends he'd ever had.

They had understood what he felt when he was on the stage. They had the same kind of focus, the same determination to be the very best they could be. Jake had never before in his life really worked at anything. But as much work as a show took, it didn't really *feel* like work. He'd been hoping camp would be like that. Now he wasn't so sure.

Destiny had wakened him at five thirty this morning, flinging himself onto Jake's bed and startling Winston, who left claw marks on Jake's bare arm as he scrambled out of Destiny's way. "Get up, get up, get up, Jake!" Destiny had hollered, prying open one of Jake's determinedly closed eyes. "It's *Eureka!* day! Finally! This is gonna be the bestest summer in my whole life!"

Jake wished he could be as sure of that as Destiny.

As he approached the door to the woodshop, Jake could hear raised voices from inside. Archie and Zedediah must still be arguing about how best to moor the dock they were working on to the land. Like the diving platform, it would be mounted on oil drums. It was designed to float so that it could accommodate itself to the water level, which changed according to how much rain they got. They'd had days and days of rain in the late spring, so the pond was unusually high. But as the summer went on, the pond would shrink.

Jake went in and found the two of them standing in their own halves of the woodshop's working space with the long, narrow, nearly completed dock between them. Each side was a reflection of father's and son's very different ways of working. On Zedediah's side the hand-tools were neatly hung on Peg-Boards, the worktable was precisely organized, with screws, nails, nuts, and bolts all in labeled containers. The wood that was destined to become the rocking chairs and gliders that made up most of his catalog was stacked neatly against the wall covered with a tarp. In the corner was a cabinet that held cans of stain, varnish, polyurethane, paint, and the solvents needed to work with them, organized by both type and size.

Archie's side was a chaos of paint cans and tools, mostly strewn on the floor, some dumped without apparent order into buckets and boxes among miscellaneous piles of oddly shaped chunks of wood and tree stumps or limbs in assorted sizes that were the raw materials from which he created his Furniture of the Absurd.

They stopped arguing when Jake came through the doorway. "What do *you* think, Jake?" Zedediah said. "Tie the dock to a couple of trees like Archie says, or sink posts a little ways back from the water and fasten it to those?"

"Whichever is easier and faster," Jake said. "Two campers are here already. E.D.'s having a fit."

"Ha!" Archie said. "Trees it is then."

"All right, trees," Zedediah conceded.

"It's awfully big," Jake said. "Will it fit through the door?"

Archie sighed. "You weren't even here for the *Incident of the Buffet!*"

Jake had heard the story, of course. Several times. When the buffet, which Archie had fashioned from the massive trunk of a fallen oak tree, was completed, it had turned out to be too long and tall and wide to get out of the shop. After a major argument about whether the buffet or the front wall of Pinewood Cottage would have to be dismantled, Archie had ended up cutting the buffet in two and turning each half into a credenza.

Zedediah claimed to have won the argument, while Archie said he'd yielded only because he realized that he could sell two pieces for more than he could have gotten for one. Zedediah always insisted that the buffet would never have sold at all. "There's a limit to how 'absurd' furniture can be and still serve any useful purpose whatsoever. That buffet wouldn't have fit into any dining room smaller than a soccer field."

"Ah, but it was a thing of beauty." Very little of Archie's furniture served a useful purpose, actually. The first piece Jake had ever seen was a coffee table that looked more like a short, fat, shiny hippopotamus. "You couldn't put a cup of coffee on it," Lucille had said of it, "but then who would want to?"

"True art is seldom practical," Archie often said.

This, Jake knew, was a thinly veiled insult aimed at Zedediah's rocking chairs. The question of who among the Applewhites created "true art" was a regular and hotly debated topic around the family dinner table. Jake had come to the conclusion that art was whatever the artist claimed it to be.

"I'll get some rope from the barn," Zedediah said, "while the two of you finish the dock. Be careful of the wet paint. Destiny decided it needed decoration."

Chapter Nine

E.D. found Cordelia and Hal in Sweet Gum Cottage, which was now the visual arts studio. Surrounded by tubes of paint, they were painting elegant wooden signs for the boys' and girls' cottages with the names of the campers who would be staying in them. It was an idea they'd thought up when everybody had still been expecting a dozen campers; and though it hardly seemed necessary now that there were only three names on each sign, they had refused to give it up. Cordelia's was covered with flowers and vines. Hal had chosen a fantasy theme of wizards and dragons and goblins. Just like them, E.D. thought, to take hours to create something only moderately useful that could have been printed out in seconds.

Paulie greeted her from his perch in the corner with a scream and a string of curses. "Hi, Paulie," she said automatically.

Hal looked up from his work. "I'm not sure I can go through with this after all. Whenever I think of staying in a cottage with three other people, I feel like I'm going to throw up."

"Quit complaining," Cordelia said. "At least you're going to have your own room, which is more than I get!"

"How long do we have till they start getting here?"

"No time at all," E.D. said. "The first two are here already. They're down in Dogwood Cottage now, complaining about the heat."

Hal's face went so white that the acne on his cheeks was more noticeable than usual. He rubbed at the sparse goatee that had taken him all spring to grow. "Now? Campers are here now? We're not ready. I'm not ready!"

"*You* don't have to be," E.D. told him. "They're Cordelia's, not yours. The Boniface twins. A really scruffy chauffeur brought them in a Mercedes! Cinnamon says they're going home, though. Between the lack of air-conditioning and the cell tower not being the right one, she is *not* a happy camper! Do you suppose we have to refund their deposit if they go home? Dad'll have a heart attack."

"Of course they're not going home," Cordelia said. "They're my first two campers! I'm so excited! Cinnamon and Ginger, right? Age eleven. The poet and—and—I forget what the other one does. I'll get right over there." She put down her paintbrush. "Could you finish painting these last two—"

E.D. just looked at her.

Cordelia picked the brush up again. "Sorry, I wasn't thinking. Would it be okay, you think, if I just take the time to paint in these lilies? It'll only take a minute."

"It isn't as if they have anywhere to go," E.D. said. "Or even any way to call home and demand their chauffeur back since their phones don't work here."

Hal put his brush down suddenly and rushed off to the bathroom. After a moment E.D. and Cordelia could hear him retching. "You think he's going to be okay?" E.D. asked.

"Of course. He only has three boys to deal with. How bad could it be?"

"It's Hal! I couldn't believe he agreed to this counselor thing in the first place."

Cordelia finished the last lily with a flourish of her brush and shrugged. "Dad had him the moment he promised to pay us! Hal was halfway through building a computerized moving sculpture when the world ended, remember? All the parts he needs to finish it cost a fortune. If he hadn't agreed to be a counselor, he'd have had to abandon the whole project."

"What are you going to do with the twins from now till the other campers come?"

Cordelia put her paintbrush into a jar of turpentine and stood up. "Don't know. I'm sure that when I meet them something will come to me. I got a zillion ideas off the internet. Like Uncle Archie says, 'Google is your friend!'" She picked up some papers from the end of the table. "These are the maps of Wit's End I made for the campers when you rejected Hal's version—"

"I didn't reject it; I gave it half the wall in the office."

"Maybe I'll give one to each of the twins and challenge them to a scavenger hunt."

"Ginger is green, Cinnamon blue," E.D. said.

"What?"

"You'll see."

"Okay." Cordelia took off her paint smock and tossed it on the end of the workbench, smoothed her long, wavy auburn hair, and tugged at the flowered skirt she had chosen to wear with her staff shirt. "Do I look all right?"

E.D. nodded. *All right?* Cordelia was flat-out gorgeous. She tended to dress like Aunt Lucille, in bright colors and flowing fabrics; but even in cutoffs and a raggedy T-shirt, she would look better than E.D. on her best day.

"Here I go. Wish me luck."

As the screen door slammed behind Cordelia, Hal came out of the bathroom wiping his mouth with the back of his hand. Paulie, preening his newly grown-in feathers, swore at him gently. "It's no good," Hal said. "I can't do this. I'll be in my room. Tell Dad I'm sorry to let the family down, but I just can't do this."

"Dad's at the airport. He'll be back in a couple of hours. The Applewhite future depends on *Eureka!* You know perfectly well you can't quit."

Hal uttered a couple of parrot words and headed back to the bathroom.

Chapter Ten

When Zedediah left, Jake and Archie went back to work on the dock. After they'd nailed the last of the top boards in place, Archie dug through a pile of scrap wood in the back corner of his side of the shop and came up with an old, paint-splattered, four-rung wooden ladder. "There weren't any more swimming pool ladders on Craigslist, so I figured we could use this."

"It won't look as classy as the other ladder."

Archie sighed. "I know—but it'll do the job." When

the dock was finished, Archie stood back to look at it. "Hardly a work of art!"

"Destiny's orange and green blotches add a nice touch," Jake said.

"It's possible that absurdity can go too far. I must remind myself that this, like the diving platform, is merely practical. Let's get a dolly under the thing and move it outside."

While they were maneuvering it through the doorway, Zedediah drove up in Archie's pickup with an enormous coil of rope in the back.

"We'll take it from here," Zedediah told Jake. "You'd better go find out what's still on E.D.'s to-do list. With her schedule screwed up like this, she's probably beside herself."

Jake headed back to the Lodge. One thing that wouldn't be on E.D.'s list was getting Winston stashed in Wisteria Cottage before anybody else arrived. Nobody understood Winston's sensitivity the way Jake did—or even noticed it particularly. But in a world as intense as the Applewhites', the dog needed his own personal safe haven. As far as Winston was concerned, that haven was Jake's bedroom—in fact, Jake's bed.

The moment Jake slipped inside the front door, Winston came running, snuffling and whining with pleasure, and leaped on him, covering his knees with saliva. "Down, boy!" Jake said, shoving the dog firmly to the floor. Winston rolled over to let Jake rub his tummy. The smell of warm chocolate wafted in from the kitchen. Lucille was making her famous triple-chocolate brownies as a treat for the first night of camp.

"Let's go," he said, "and get you stowed." But outside, instead of heading for Wisteria Cottage, Winston trotted purposefully off toward the meadow, his tail waving cheerily. Jake didn't whistle him back. If the dog wanted a walk, why not let him have one before he got cooped up in his safe haven?

Winston leaped at a butterfly—the only prey he ever went after—prey he never came anywhere near catching. It was funny to watch the big, ungainly basset hound leap up in the air after a butterfly that could float effortlessly out of his reach. For some reason, Winston never got discouraged. *Butterfly, leap. Butterfly, leap.*

Across the meadow, Winston took the woods trail in under the trees. Jake followed, watching his footing to keep from tripping over wisteria vines or the things E.D. called barbed wire vine. Lucille said they were greenbrier, but E.D. insisted that nothing as vicious as that should have such a pretty name. No matter how often the vines were cut back from the trail, they grew across it again. In spite of that, the trail was passable—cutting cross-country through the woods was nearly impossible. Between wisteria, barbed wire vine, and poison ivy, the North Carolina woods could be treacherous, but at least they were quiet and shady. Jake began to hum "Consider Yourself at Home," his favorite song from *Oliver!*. His heart lifted immediately. *This*, Jake thought, *is what Zedediah means when he talks about joy*. In no time he had switched from humming to singing, his voice filling the green shade of the woods.

When he finished the song, he thought he heard voices from the general direction of the pond. He stopped and listened. Girls' voices. The fur rose along Winston's back, and he began making the whuffling sound he made when he was deciding whether to bark. It couldn't be E.D. or Cordelia. Winston never whuffled at anyone he knew. It had to be the twins.

"No worries," he told the dog. "We don't have to go anywhere near the pond." He had taken only a few more steps along the trail when there was a bloodcurdling shriek. It was followed by another, and another. Soon there were two voices shrieking. Whatever was going on, it sounded serious.

Jake tore through the woods toward the pond, leaping over vines and fallen limbs, shoving branches out of his way as he went, his skin getting scraped by the thorns of the barbed wire vine. Winston lumbered behind him, barking frantically. When Jake emerged from under the trees, he saw one of the twins, completely covered with black muck, standing hip deep in the pond. Her carroty curls had vanished under the muck, as had her freckles. The only part of her that wasn't black was her mouth, stretched wide in yet another scream. The other twin, in a blue swimsuit, was dancing along the edge of the pond, staying well back from the edge, her bare feet, too, black with muck.

"Come back!" the blue twin yelled. "Right this minute! Come back here!"

"I can't! I can't! It's got me. I can't move! You gotta come pull me out!" The muck-covered twin held a dripping hand out to her sister. *"Quick, quick! It's sucking me down! I'm gonna drown!"*

"I can't come out there. It'll get me too. We'll both drown!"

Jake sighed. The girls had begun to cry now, growing more hysterical by the minute. He pulled off his sneakers and socks, ran to the pond, and splashed into the water, sinking deeper into the mud with every step he took. It was all he could do to keep his balance as he pulled one foot after another out of the mire.

Good thing she's so small, he thought. She was still gasping through her sobs that she was drowning when he reached her, pulled her free, and threw her, dripping slime, over his shoulder. Slight as she was, the extra weight forced him even farther into the mud. Still, he managed to slog his way back to shore without falling in himself. No way this girl had been in any danger of being pulled under.

"You saved me, you saved me," she was saying as he set her down on the grass.

Jake wrinkled his nose. The feel of the muck didn't particularly bother him underfoot, but the smell was disgusting: all mold and rot and dead things. Dead fishy things. He was almost as black with it now as the girl.

The other twin had started screaming again. She was sitting among the cattails at the edge of the pond, trying to fend Winston off as he slathered her face with his tongue. Jake didn't need to have seen it to know what had happened. Winston couldn't stand to see anyone cry, stranger or not. He always did his best to offer comfort, which consisted of licking them reassuringly. And thoroughly. He must have jumped on her and knocked her backward.

Jake went over, grabbed Winston's collar, and pulled him away.

"That's it!" the girl said, struggling to her feet and trying to wipe Winston's saliva off her face with one hand and the mud off her bottom with the other. "Get me to a phone," she demanded. "Right now! My sister and I are going home."

Jake picked up a towel that was crumpled on the grass. He supposed the girls had been intending to swim out to the diving platform that floated invitingly in the center of the pond. Kids who were used to swimming pools clearly didn't understand about ponds. He took the towel over to the other girl, who was trying unsuccessfully to clean her face with her muddy hands.

"How'd you fall down?" he asked as she began toweling her face and hair.

She looked up at him, her eyes wide. "I didn't *fall*. It was the pond! It's like something out of Stephen King. I just started walking out into it, and it pulled me in, knocked me over, and started to suck me down. I was lucky to get up again." She dropped the towel and threw her arms around him. "Thank you, thank you. You saved my life!"

It was then that Cordelia arrived. "I see you've met Jake." Jake disentangled himself from the mud-covered twin. "What are you two doing here? You're supposed to be on a scavenger hunt over by the barn!"

"It's too hot for a scavenger hunt," the muddy twin said.

"Besides," the other one added, "I never compete with Ginger. There's no point. She always wins. We saw the pond on the map you gave us and decided to swim instead."

This, Jake thought, was why they'd all been warned never to let the campers out of their sight.

"Our father is going to sue you for everything you've got!" the green twin said. "How come you didn't warn us about this death pond?"

Cordelia smiled a bright and entirely unconvincing smile. "How come you didn't notice the sign in your bunk that says, No Swimming Without a Lifeguard Present?"

"Get me to a phone," said the blue twin. "Now! We're going home!"

"If you say so," Cordelia said, "but you have to come to the office to use the phone, and you're not setting foot in the office till you've had a shower. Besides, you're going to need some lunch. We hadn't expected to have campers here till dinnertime, but I make a mean peanut butter sandwich."

From the look on the girls' faces, Jake figured peanut butter sandwiches were not a staple of their diet. "Let's go, Winston," he said, picking up his socks and shoving his muddy feet into his sneakers.

The sound of Archie's pickup heralded the arrival of the floating dock as Cordelia shepherded the muddy twins back toward their bunk.

Chapter Eleven

1:55 P.M. Camper-arrival time minus five. E.D., standing on the Lodge porch, pinned her EXECUTIVE ASSISTANT name tag to her staff T-shirt, scanned her clipboard, and sighed with relief. In spite of the rocky start to this day, things seemed now to be under control. A long metal folding table had been put up in front of the two Zedediah Applewhite rocking chairs. REGISTRATION, said the paper taped to the front of it in large, plain block letters. E.D. had made that herself. Taped to the top of the table so it wouldn't blow away was a spreadsheet with the names of the campers and their parents' names, addresses, phone numbers, and e-mail addresses, with boxes for checking off each of the campers as they arrived. She'd checked off Cinnamon and Ginger before she printed it. Four water bottles were lined up next to four canvas bags, and there was a plastic bin for collecting camper cell phones. On the far end of the table were the maps Cordelia had made.

Cordelia, E.D. thought, was a genius. Once the twins had recovered from the disaster at the pond, she had somehow managed to keep them occupied and away from the phone. Grandpa and Uncle Archie had put the new dock in place, tied to a pair of sweet gum trees and connected to solid ground by a wooden ramp. An hour ago her father had called from the airport to report that Samantha Peterman's flight had arrived on time, and she and Destiny were having lunch. "Destiny, of course, is talking her ears off," Randolph had said, "but she's doing her best to hide behind a book. It's a good thing Quincy Brown's plane gets in at two. Destiny has already filled up the drawing pad he brought along."

Her mother and Aunt Lucille had finished everything that could be done ahead of time for tonight's opening dinner and had gone off to change so they'd be ready to greet the campers as they arrived. Jake had finished the last-minute chores E.D. had given him. She herself had made and put out cardboard signs along the drive with arrows pointing to Camp Registration, because Hal, whose job that was supposed to be, had closed himself in his old bedroom and was refusing to come out.

The screen door banged, and her mother emerged from the house. She was wearing the khaki shorts and shirt outfit she had bought years ago for a safari to research *Petunia Grantham on the Veldt*. On one of the many shirt pockets was pinned her name tag, SYBIL JAMESON, AUTHOR AND ASSOCIATE CAMP DIRECTOR. Her jaw was clenched with determination. Aunt Lucille came hurrying around the house now from Wisteria Cottage, dressed in a swirly skirt and flowered blouse, her curls falling loose and beginning to frizz. Her name tag said simply LUCILLE APPLEWHITE, POET. "This is so exciting!" The arrival of the evil twins did not seem to have dampened her enthusiasm. "Everything ready?" she asked brightly.

Before E.D. could answer, they heard, out beyond the bushes, a car turning into the driveway. Two o'clock, E.D. noted. Whoever this was, they were impeccably on time. Aunt Lucille and her mother took their seats behind the registration table. An ancient, battered Volkswagen bus came around the curve of the drive and pulled to a stop in front of the porch with a squeal of brakes. The driver's door opened, and a woman in cutoffs and a tank top, with a long brown braid reaching halfway down her back, jumped out.

E.D. had never seen anyone like her. Except for her face, every square inch of visible skin was covered with brilliantly colored tattoos. There were horses with flowing manes and tails ridden by figures that could have been humans or spirits, warriors or elves. There were dragons and flowers and strange, calligraphic symbols. The woman was a walking art gallery.

"Out, Harley!" the woman called. "I have to be in Asheville in time for setup."

This, E.D. realized, was Marlie Michaels, lead singer of Dragon's Breath and mother of Harley Schobert, age twelve. The other door opened then, and Harley slid down from the passenger seat. He had medium long, medium brown hair and a medium face on a medium body. He was wearing blue running shorts, a plain white T-shirt, and sneakers. In a crowd of kids—any kids—this boy, E.D. thought, would completely disappear. Marlie Michaels and Harley Schobert, mother and son. It was as if a starling egg had been slipped into a bird of paradise nest by mistake.

As Harley and his mother went up the porch steps to the registration table, E.D. heard another car on the driveway. This would be David Giacomo, she thought.

A dark red sedan pulled up behind the van. The woman who emerged from the driver's side—dark hair perfectly styled, wearing a yellow-and-white sundress and white, strappy sandals—was staring at Marlie Michaels with an expression of horror. E.D. wondered whether she might be at that very moment changing her mind about leaving her son at *Eureka!* That was to be the last rational thought that went through E.D.'s mind that afternoon. Because just then David Giacomo stepped out of the car.

The photo he'd sent with his camp application had shown him to be good-looking. But this kid was not good-looking. This kid was—E.D. searched for a word that fit—*awesome*, that was it. Not the way her friend Melissa used it, for everything from a lipstick color to a hamburger, but for what the word really meant: "inspiring amazement and respect, combined with a feeling of personal powerlessness." That was it exactly. His longish, wavy, blue-black hair framed a face with a straight nose, high cheekbones, full lips, and large, wide-set eyes—eyes that were startlingly blue. She had seen a face like that somewhere before, but where?

David Giacomo was tall. He was slim. Ethereal. Absolutely awesome! There was a kind of glow around him—like an angel. Suddenly she knew where she had seen a face like this before: in the research for her spring semester paper on Renaissance art. David Giacomo was a Botticelli angel! E.D. felt like a little pile of iron filings, pulled inexorably toward a magnet.

He was fourteen. But he looked older. She reminded

herself to breathe. Then she hurried to the registration table, picked up a canvas bag and a water bottle, and took them to him. She was aware that the adults were talking, that David was answering a question. His voice was soft and smooth and resonant. She handed him the bag. As he took it, his long fingers brushed hers, and a tiny electrical shock traveled all the way down to her toes.

"E.D.! E.D.! Your phone!"

Her mother's voice penetrated her consciousness, and E.D. became aware that the cell phone in her shorts pocket was playing Reveille—her father's ring. "Excuse me," she said. "I should take this." A moment later she found herself behind the house, out of earshot, though she didn't remember walking away from the porch.

"Disaster!" her father yelled the moment she answered. She held the phone away from her ear. "Complete catastrophe! Quincy's plane has been delayed. Some nonsense about an equipment malfunction. Do they expect me to believe there is only one plane they could possibly send here from Atlanta?" With the image of David Giacomo filling her mind, E.D. found herself listening to her father's rant with surprising calm.

"The idiot agent I was talking to actually called security on me. They accused me of *shouting*, if you'd believe it. All I did was very calmly and entirely rationally mention the possibility of a lawsuit. They threatened to kick me out of the airport. If Destiny hadn't started crying, they might have done it. They left one of the security guards to keep an eye on me. They say it'll be another three hours at least! Samantha's finished her book. And what am I going to do with Destiny? He's talking to the guard now. Asking questions. You know how Destiny can get on a person's nerves—the man has a gun, for heaven's sake."

"Take Destiny to the gift shop," E.D. said. "Buy him a new sketch pad. Maybe some new markers."

Before her father could say anything else, she told him a camper was arriving and she had to go. She flipped her phone shut. Her father was a grown-up, she thought. He could surely cope for a few more hours.

By the time she had hurried back around to the porch, the van had gone and her mother was deep in conversation with David's mother. David himself had disappeared, as had Harley. Her heart sank. "Where did he—*they*—go?" she asked Aunt Lucille, an odd quiver in her voice.

"Jake came and took them off to the boys' bunk. I'm going to go up and see if I can pry Hal out of his room."

"I'd better go make sure everything is okay over there," E.D. said.

The rest of the afternoon passed in a blur of images with David Giacomo in the center. There were two more frantic phone calls from the airport. Later, Cordelia, Ginger, and Cinnamon appeared with a bucket of homemade bubble mix and a handful of enormous wands they had made out of wire coat hangers, and challenged the boys to see who could make the biggest bubbles. David could, it turned out. *Of course*, E.D. thought. She remembered David's application. Zedediah had called him a "Renaissance man." David, apparently, could do anything.

At some point Cordelia organized a scavenger hunt with the rule that no one was allowed to go near the pond. "As if!" said the green twin. Cordelia had neglected, however, to warn the campers about the goats. So the scavenger hunt had been interrupted by a hysterical chase, first Wolfie chasing campers and then most of the Applewhites chasing Wolfie. David ran not only extremely fast, E.D. noticed, but with the grace of a dancer.

The campers were just bringing the last of their scavenger hunt finds to the Lodge porch when Randolph finally drove up in Sybil's station wagon.

Destiny bounded out of the car the instant it stopped. "Daddy almost gotted put in jail!" he shouted. "I was scared for a little bit, except the guard guy was really nice. He's got goatses at home, just like us, but no dog and no parrot. And then Q came—his name's really Quincy, but he calls himself Q—and you know what he did?" Destiny didn't so much as take a breath before he answered his own question. "He gotted everybody dancing. Practically everybody in the whole airport!"

Randolph, Samantha Peterman, and Quincy Brown had gotten out of the car now as well. "Not so many," Quincy said, flashing a 500-watt smile. "The flight attendant just asked me to show what I did in Atlanta after they announced the delay."

"Destiny's almost right," Randolph said. "He even got that security guard dancing. Show them, Q."

The boy began stomping his feet on the gravel drive, slapping his hands on his legs, and clapping in an intricate pattern, slowly at first, then picking up speed.

"It's called Step!" Destiny said. "Isn't it great? I can do the hands and the feet both! He showed me while we was waiting for the suitcases to come!" He joined in now, stamping and slapping and clapping.

"In Atlanta, when they said they didn't have a plane for us, people started to get ugly," Quincy said when the routine was finished. "My grandfather says Step is good for cheering people up, so I started to do some. Pretty soon a couple of guys joined in. And then some more. People started coming to watch from whole different concourses! By the time they'd found us a plane, there were old ladies clapping and stomping and a whole traveling baseball team using the trash cans for hand drums. The guys from the airline said they never saw people so happy about a delay in their lives! Somebody videoed it with his phone and said he's gonna post it online!"

As everyone else hurried over to greet the newcomers, E.D. found herself edging closer to David, who remained where he'd been during Q's performance, leaning elegantly against the porch railing, his arms crossed, a half smile on his face.

Chapter Twelve

At dinner, which was more than an hour late thanks to the plane delay, the boys all sat at one picnic table in the dining tent—except Hal, who took his food and sneaked off to his room—and the girls at another. Samantha brought a book with her and read steadily while she ate. Ginger, Jake noticed, kept her eyes fixed on him. Whenever he glanced that way, she broke into a toothy grin.

Destiny, at the boys' table, asked question after question, barely giving the guys time to answer before he was on to the next. He wanted to know where Q had learned to do Step. How come he lived with his grandfather instead of his mother and father and whether they had a cottage like Zedediah's, or a parrot. How many floors there were in his apartment building. What it was like to live where you had to ride in an elevator to get home. Q just kept eating and answering till Destiny switched to Harley.

He wanted to know how come Harley was wearing a camera around his neck and was he going to take pictures of everything they did at camp and how come he didn't like taking pictures of people and why wasn't he eating any of Aunt Lucille's best-brownies-in-the-whole-world-ever.

When he started on David, David didn't answer. So Destiny just asked louder, till finally David told him to shut up and let him eat. This was surprising, Jake thought. People were almost never rude to Destiny. But Destiny was undaunted. "You don't gots to stop eating. It's not polite to *talk* with your mouth full, but it's okay to listen."

David was the only one at the boys' table who didn't find that funny.

The tour of Wit's End that was supposed to have happened before dinner had been postponed until afterward. If Jake had known Ginger was going to be at his heels the whole time, he would have excused himself and gone to hide out in his room, like Hal.

85

Every time he turned around, there she was, staring up at him. Twice he practically stepped on her.

It was almost nine, and Destiny had been sent, protesting, to bed, before they finally gathered everybody together at the campfire circle for the Opening Ceremony. The fire and marshmallow-toasting part of the plan had already been canceled because of heat and lack of time, and Zedediah had asked that all the welcoming speeches be cut as short as possible.

Again, as the campers went to find seats on the logs around the circle, the girls headed one way and the boys another. But as soon as Jake sat, Ginger scurried over and sat beside him—very, very close beside him. The night was hot enough, but she was like a little radiator. He could feel the sweat running down the middle of his back.

Zedediah spoke very briefly about the critical importance of creativity in human civilization and the intention for *Eureka!* to become a "true creative community—one for all and all for one." Randolph, however, took nearly half an hour to extol the virtues of theater—"the single art that includes all the rest." Jake wondered what his talk might have been like if he hadn't been asked to cut it short. Hal, on the other hand, was done in about ten seconds. He stood up, said he would be doing visual arts with an emphasis on painting, and sat down again.

Jake was after Hal. As he moved to get up, Ginger

grabbed for his hand. She pressed a folded piece of paper into his palm, closed his fingers over it, and let go. *Now what?* Jake thought. He stuck the paper in his pocket and went to the center of the circle. "I'm not much for speeches," he said, "but I'll be leading the singing workshop. Who here knows 'Doe a Deer,' from *The Sound of Music?*" When they raised their hands, he started the campers singing it. Unlike the Applewhites, the kids could carry a tune. Q sang every bit as well as he danced. David was good, too, but he sang louder than the others instead of trying to blend in with them. The only camper he couldn't tell anything about was Harley, who had sat bent over his camera through the whole thing and didn't sing at all. When the song was over, Jake went to the other side of the circle and sat next to Archie instead of where he'd been before.

By the time the campers were dismissed to their bunks to get ready for bed, it was 9:55, so Jake went to the Lodge, where a staff meeting was supposed to begin at ten. Nobody was in the living room when he got there. He pulled the paper Ginger had given him out of his pocket and sat down on the couch.

MY SAVIOR, JAKE SEMPLE

Nearly sucked to my doom
In the foul-smelling gloom,
I was crying, crying, crying,
Nearly dying, dying, dying!

But Jake came along
With his muscles so strong
And lifted me free,
Saving me, saving me!

Before camp could start
Jake had captured my heart.

It was printed in red marker and signed *Your FF,*
Ginger Boniface. There was an entire row of *x*'s and *o*'s
across the bottom. Jake groaned and stuffed it back
into his pocket. He had no tools for dealing with
something like this.

A few minutes later, Sybil came in to call Jake outside
to the dining tent. "There's been an insurrection!"

The campers, it turned out, had flatly rejected the
idea of roughing it. David, citing extreme sensitivity,
announced that if he and Quincy—David insisted on
using Q's full name—didn't get a fan in their room, he
would "die in the night from suffocation and heat
prostration." *Extreme sensitivity!* Jake thought. Sure.
David had made a fuss at dinner because there was no
vegetarian option. As much attention as Q got just
being his incredibly outgoing, incredibly positive self,
David was probably just trying to get somebody
besides E.D. to notice him. She'd been practically
drooling over the kid all day. Jake couldn't imagine
what she saw in him.

After that, of course, everybody demanded fans, including Hal and Cordelia. Jake and Archie were sent to the barn to see whether there were any fans left over from before air-conditioning. They located four, which were provided to the campers. Archie had to promise Hal and Cordelia that he would drive to town first thing in the morning to get two more.

Then there was the issue of whether individual reading lights could be kept on after lights-out, which Samantha Peterman insisted was absolutely necessary (*no*) and whether campers could listen to their personal music with earbuds after lights-out (*yes*— after Randolph, who maintained that it led to deafness and interfered with brain waves, had been argued down by Zedediah).

After that there was another uproar because the twins had discovered that the Wi-Fi in the Lodge didn't reach the cottages; not only did their phones not work, but they couldn't get online in their room. Cinnamon once again demanded a telephone to arrange to be taken home. Sybil, who by that time had lost whatever patience she'd been able to muster, informed her that only emergency phone calls could be made after ten and when Cinnamon claimed that this *was* an emergency, made up a rule on the spot that an emergency required a fever, severe bleeding, or vomiting.

Finally there was the question of whether, if they

kept the lights out, the campers could stay up talking and maybe hang out in the living rooms of the cottages (*most definitely not*). Whether the campers talked in their rooms or not (*quietly—in whispers— with no singing and no loud laughter*) was up to them, but they were to be in their beds at the stroke of ten with all lights out—except for this first night—and they were to stay there till wake-up call at 7:30 A.M.

Jake was nearly asleep on his feet by the time Randolph called the staff back to the Lodge for the staff meeting.

Chapter Thirteen

Everyone still had their official name tags on, E.D. noticed, when they were finally settled in the living room of the Lodge. The only staff members missing were Hal, Visual Artist/Counselor, and Cordelia, Dancer/Counselor, who were in the bunks watching over the hot, tired, and grumpy campers.

Randolph Applewhite, Camp Director, beamed around at the others. "All in all, an auspicious beginning. *Eureka!* is off to a brilliant start!" This was a stretch even for an Applewhite. E.D. had been expecting something more like "What have we gotten ourselves into?"

"I would hardly call it brilliant," Sybil said. "Dinner was a catastrophe. The twins demanded whole wheat buns for their barbecue, and Harley doesn't like chocolate. What kind of kid doesn't like chocolate? David is a vegetarian and can't stand Kool-Aid, and—"

"You should have put a question on the application about food issues," Randolph said.

"We *did*!" E.D. said.

"David apparently only decided he was a vegetarian the day before yesterday! We've got to redo all the menus and go shopping again. Whole wheat buns? Whatever happened to kids who live on hot dogs, peanut butter, and chicken nuggets?"

Her mother had only agreed to share the job of cooking with Aunt Lucille, E.D. knew, because she'd been shamed into it by Randolph.

Jake Semple, Singing Coach, stifled a yawn. Even stifled, it was contagious. E.D. yawned and so did her grandfather. It was now well after eleven. Archie Applewhite, Sculptor, sitting on the couch with his head on Aunt Lucille's shoulder, appeared to have fallen asleep. Paulie stood on one foot on his perch, his beak tucked under his wing, Winston was snoring noisily at Jake's feet, and Destiny Applewhite, Camp Mascot, was surely doing the same in his bed upstairs. E.D. envied them.

"Things could have been worse," her father said now.

Her mother wasn't buying it. "Besides the food disaster," she said, "we've got a kid who threatens to go home every time something doesn't suit her—"

"Just don't let her get to a phone!"

"—and a mother who has already called four times to find out if her kid's okay."

"Which mother?" Lucille asked.

"Samantha's. Turns out the child has never been away from home overnight."

"That explains it! When the insurrection started, she came to me crying and begging me to let her call home."

"Bad idea!" Randolph said. "If we let the girl talk to her mother, they'll just stir each other up all the more. Next thing you know that child will be on a plane headed home. We are not going to lose a camper!"

"Never mind," Lucille said. "I gave her some breathing exercises and told her to give herself three days. By that time she'll be all caught up in camp activities. It's just homesickness. She'll be fine."

"And I explained to Mrs. Peterman the last time she called," Sybil said, "that we'd call *her* if there were any problems. We nearly lost a camper before he even registered. Mrs. Giacomo practically had a heart attack when she saw Marlie Michaels's tattoos. I had to do some fast talking, let me tell you! It's a good

93

thing *Harley* looked normal or David would have been back in Virginia by now."

Randolph slammed his hand down on the arm of the couch. "We aren't refunding deposits! No matter what. The income from this benighted idea is barely enough as it is."

Apparently her father had forgotten for the moment whose benighted idea it was, E.D. thought. At least he had come back from whatever rosy fantasy land he was inhabiting when the meeting started. If they were going to save Wit's End, they all had to gut this out no matter what it meant, but there was no point in pretending it was going to be easy.

"We need to talk about Community Service," E.D. said now. "Nobody mentioned it at the Opening Ceremony." She held up the stapled schedules she was planning to give the family tonight and hand out to the campers in the morning. "It's all here, and after seeing how they reacted to the idea of roughing it, I think when they find out about Community Service, we could have another insurrection on our hands."

During the weeks of planning for camp, E.D. had been the first to realize that all the usual chores that kept Wit's End livable would still need to be done. The jobs like laundry and cleaning, vacuuming and dusting had always been a source of considerable conflict in the family. No one liked doing them, and what they didn't like, they tended to avoid whenever possible.

From time to time Wit's End had, in fact, become very nearly *un*livable. That couldn't happen with people paying big money for their kids to be here.

Besides that, having six more people in residence and two more cottages lived in regularly meant that there would be even greater-than-usual need for most of these chores, so E.D. had come up with the idea of simply including them in the camp schedule. Each camper would be assigned a particular chore every day. "Calling this stuff Community Service should help support the whole 'all for one and one for all' thing," she'd said.

Lucille had agreed. "We will appeal to their higher natures." It had seemed a better idea at the time than it did now.

In her welcoming talk Lucille had mentioned that all beds were to be made each morning and the bunks straightened before her prebreakfast Welcome-the-Day Meditation and Yoga activity. There had been considerable groaning among the campers even at this. Community Service included plenty of worse jobs: cleaning bathrooms, setting up for meals, helping with dishes, weeding the vegetable garden, feeding the goats, cutting the grass.

"We should just spring their assignments on them every morning at breakfast," Sybil said. "That'll keep them off balance. These are intelligent and creative kids. Give them too much time, and they'll figure out a way around actually doing anything."

"Off balance!" Randolph said then. "That's an excellent idea. We should spring the *whole schedule* on them a day at a time. It will encourage flexibility, one of the prime traits of the creative individual. Each camper will have to begin the day ready for anything."

E.D. thought of the effort and the time—days and days—she had put into creating the camp schedule for the whole eight weeks. The schedule, in its three-ring binder, was on top of a filing cabinet in the office. She had with her now the first week—three-and-a-half double-sided pages stapled together. They were neatly laid out, spreadsheet fashion, with workshops color coded for easy reference.

She had begun to think of the whole thing as a work of art, an absolutely practical work of art. The colors provided continuity for the whole eight weeks, even as daily schedules varied. Morning workshops and evening activities (*all required for all campers*) were in red, mealtimes in yellow, optional afternoon workshops in green, water activities in blue, and free time in purple. Staff members each had an icon— theater masks for Randolph, quill pen for Lucille, pencil for Sybil, musical note for Jake, ballet slippers for Cordelia, paintbrush for Hal, saw for Zedediah, and chisel for Archie. These icons, in the upper left corners of the color blocks, showed who was in charge of the activity.

Aunt Lucille reached over and patted E.D.'s hand. "Don't worry, sweetie, everybody knows what a great job you did with the schedule. The only thing that's changing here is when the campers see it."

Zedediah yawned again. "Everybody remember, it's only the first day." He looked at his watch. "Closing in on becoming the second. Staff meeting or no staff meeting, I'm going to bed. There's nothing more we can accomplish here tonight." With that, the old man pushed himself up from his chair and went over to Paulie's perch. "Bedtime, fella," he said, holding out his arm.

The parrot ruffled his feathers, stepped onto Zedediah's arm, and made his way up to his shoulder. "Night, night," the bird said. E.D. had a feeling, sometimes, that Paulie knew exactly what he was saying.

In the doorway, Zedediah turned back for a moment. "You did a fine job with the schedule, E.D. Give them just one day of it tomorrow, and we'll see what happens. We'll all have to take this a day at a time, you know. I have great faith that this family can accomplish whatever we set our minds to do—even if it *was* Randolph's idea. See you at breakfast."

"Oh, my God, breakfast!" Sybil said as Zedediah left. "*Breakfast!* I promised the twins stone-ground whole wheat bread by morning! And whatever will we do for lunch?"

Archie opened his eyes and stretched his arms over

his head. "I'm going to town for fans first thing. I'll stop at the grocery store while I'm there—just give me a list." He glanced around the room, saw that Zedediah was no longer there, and turned to Lucille. "I'm wiped. Let's go."

"All right, all right," Randolph said. "Meeting's over."

E.D. sighed. She couldn't go to bed till she'd printed out six copies of only the first day's schedule.

Chapter Fourteen

I t was only 7:45, and already the day was hot and muggy. After Destiny had been forbidden to go to Lucille's first Meditation and Yoga session, Jake had brought him to the goat pen. Jake had, of course, shut Wolfie and his food into the shed, because Destiny had been chased so often he had nightmares about brown-and-white monsters with huge lopsided horns.

Now Destiny was grumbling as he scooped feed into Hazel's plastic bucket. "I don't see how comes I don't get to do what the campers do," Destiny said.

"What's a mascot anyway? Doesn't mascots get to *do* anything?"

"You get to do things," Jake said. "You have a Community Service job every single day, just like everybody else. Today you and I both have goat duty."

"That's not a *camp* thing. We gots to do that all the time. I wanna do what Aunt Lucille's doing in the barn."

"It's just for campers."

"E.D.'s there, and she's not a camper."

"What can I tell you, kid? Life's not fair. Besides, it's meditation. You know you don't do meditation. You always talk the whole time."

"Sometimes I sing!"

"Right. Singing's good, but it's not meditation. Maybe, if you ask nicely and promise not to talk during it, Lucille will let you do the yoga part after today. They'll do that outside. It's the sun salutation."

"I *like* yoga," Destiny said. "I do downward-facing dog real good."

"You do. But you'd have to promise not to bark. *Listen*, Destiny—even if your aunt lets you do yoga with the campers, you're still not going to get to go to the workshops with them."

Hazel came over to get her breakfast, and Destiny patted her head. "Well, it's not fair. There's all these new kids here—I don't hardly ever get to see new kids—and nobody's letting me be with 'em!"

Jake sighed. Home schooling was a really good thing in some ways, but maybe not so much for a kid like Destiny. The more people there were for him to talk to, the happier he was, and the easier it was on everybody. "Tell you what. My workshop's about singing. If your parents say it's okay, you can come to that."

"Yay, Jake! I loves to sing. Singing makes my heart feel good."

Jake laughed. "Mine too." He ushered Destiny out of the goat pen, opened the door of the shed, sprinted across the pen, and slammed the gate behind him moments before Wolfie crashed into the fence. "Let's go back and see what's for breakfast."

"Maybe it's waffles! Waffles is the best of best."

As they came around the side of the Lodge, Jake heard a vehicle slowing down out on the road. "Archie must be back from town," he said to Destiny. "He went to get groceries."

Destiny stopped and listened. "Nope. That doesn't sound like the truck."

"Maybe he took your mom's car."

They could hear it turning into the driveway now, tires crunching on the gravel. After a moment it stopped, its engine idling.

"How comes he stopped?" Destiny asked. "Let's go see if he brung waffles for breakfast."

The car Jake and Destiny saw when they got

around the row of bushes wasn't Sybil's. It was a plain, black compact. As soon as the driver saw them, he threw the car into reverse, backed hurriedly onto the road, and roared away.

"Who was that?" Destiny asked. "Hardly nobody ever comes down that road."

Jake shrugged. "Or into the drive. Maybe he was lost."

"I coulda told him where he was. Mommy made me learn our address. Did you know our road doesn't even gots a name? Just a number."

"He was probably using the driveway to turn around."

"No, Jake. 'Cause when he went away I heard him goin' the same way he was already goin' before."

Destiny was right, Jake realized. He was one sharp kid.

"Look, look!" Destiny said, "Uncle Archie's truck's over by the tent. Let's go see if he brung waffles."

Chapter Fifteen

On the stage floor in the barn, Cordelia and the campers were sitting cross-legged— Samantha in full lotus position—in a circle around Lucille. Cinnamon was in blue again, Ginger in green. Q and David sat together, elbowing each other from time to time. Harley, a camera on a strap around his neck, was staring fixedly at something on the floor in front of him. E.D. had slipped in late and was standing in the shadows by the stage door, leaning against the rough barn siding. Hal must have skipped out again, she thought, till she saw him in the back corner of the stage, his eyes already closed, probably pretending he was alone in a cave somewhere.

"Stillness is essential to the creative imagination," Lucille was saying now. "That's why we don't allow cell phones at *Eureka!* All the electronic technology we're surrounded with fractures our attention."

"Huh!" Cinnamon snorted.

Lucille went on as if she hadn't heard. "Meditation can mend that fractured consciousness. So now, if you are comfortable with it, close your eyes."

As far as E.D. could tell, most of the campers did that. Cinnamon, however, sat with her arms crossed in front of her, fingers tapping her upper arms, frowning into the shadows above the rows of theater seats.

"Become aware of the air moving in through your nostrils. Now, let it out again, with a gentle sigh, through your mouth." Lucille closed her eyes as well. "Try breathing that way for three minutes, keeping your attention on your breath. Feel the air moving in—out—in—out. Feel it. Listen to it. Let your mind go still."

Lucille had been trying to find a way to help E.D. meditate for years now. Sometimes, she said, instead of closing your eyes, you could still your mind by focusing your attention on something beautiful. A candle flame. A mandala. A lotus. E.D. focused her attention on David, watching his shoulders and chest rise and fall with his breath. A thin shaft of sunlight shone between the boards of the barn wall and fell on his dark, wavy hair. E.D. began to imagine that light expanding until it surrounded him with a pale, golden aura. Little by little, the aura seemed to become real, growing around him with each breath. Stillness. E.D. smiled. She had achieved stillness!

Did angels have to breathe, she wondered suddenly. Did they have lungs? Botticelli, she knew, had painted his angels from human models, but did real angels have real bodies? Or weren't they real at all? Were they just figments of human imagination? David, of course, was no figment. . . .

A brilliant flash shattered the moment. Everybody's eyes were open now.

"Harley! No, no, no! There will be no cameras in morning meditation!" Lucille held her hand out. After a moment the boy took the strap off over his head and handed her his camera, muttering about the beautiful dead beetle he'd found.

"Can we be done?" Cinnamon asked. "My butt hurts."

"Maybe we could bring pillows next time," Samantha said.

"If you focus on your breath, you'll find that after a while you don't even notice the floor," Lucille said.

E.D. had tried this. It never really worked for her.

The floor was the floor. Apparently it hadn't worked for anyone else, either. The others had begun groaning and fidgeting now, so Lucille announced they could all get up and go outside. "Meditation takes practice. In fact, it *is* a practice. We'll start every morning this way"—Cinnamon sighed dramatically—"and you'll get the hang of it soon enough. Three minutes at first, then five, then ten; believe me, meditation will enhance your creativity and defuse stress. It will be a useful tool the rest of your life." She pushed herself up from the floor. "Everybody up! Let's go salute the glorious sun and get those bodies awake and energized and flexible. Balance, campers! Mind, body, spirit."

E.D. slipped out the door. If there was one thing she liked less than meditation, it was yoga. Her body was *not* flexible. Aunt Lucille—Cordelia too—could bend over at the waist and put their hands absolutely flat on the floor. E.D. had never gotten farther than her ankles. Even Jake did better at yoga than she did. She headed for the kitchen to get something to eat before she had to hand out the schedules in the dining tent.

Three hours later she was tromping through the woods in search of a missing camper. She should have realized that things had started off too well. There had been no rebellion at all about the first Community Service assignments. She had attributed that partly to assigning only easy chores this first day—no bathroom cleaning—but mostly to the fact that it was Zedediah, with his white hair and mustache and that natural air of authority, who had explained the concept. Not even the Boniface girls had raised a complaint, though Cordelia had told her at breakfast that she'd had to teach them how to make their beds. "Can you believe they'd never done it before?"

After that, the first required workshop, Archie's Introduction to Natural Materials Sculpture, went well. E.D. attended, having decided that *Eureka!* needed a historian—someone to observe and take notes so there would be a record of what worked and what didn't, in case, against all sanity, they ever decided to do this again. As historian, of course, her iron-filing self would have an excuse to hang out around David-the-magnet. It made her heart beat faster, somehow, just to be in the same room with him. The second workshop had been Poetry. She hadn't been able to go to that one because Sybil needed her in the kitchen.

That was how she had missed the moment when things went wrong. Lucille had asked the campers to write a poem in their journals—a poem about the first feelings they'd had when they woke up that morning—and Cinnamon had said she needed to go back to Dogwood for a different pen. "I write better in color."

Lucille, of course, allowed her to go. Cinnamon had not returned. After ten minutes Lucille considered sending Ginger after her sister, but Ginger was writing steadily and furiously in her journal and Lucille didn't want to interrupt. So she had simply continued her workshop, assuming that Cinnamon would show up at any moment. She did not.

Nor, when the workshop was over, was she found in Dogwood, in any of the bathrooms, at the pond, in the Lodge, or in any of the other cottages. E.D. had been sent to wake up her father, who was seldom functional till noon.

"Missing?" Uncharacteristically, he had leaped out of bed so fast that he had a dizzy spell and had to hold onto her shoulder for a moment. "A camper is missing? Don't tell the other campers," he said, running a hand through his sleep-tousled hair.

"They already know," E.D. said. "They were all in the workshop she didn't come back to."

"Then get the campers busy doing something and get everybody else out there searching. We have to find her! Now!" He grabbed for his jeans. "We simply cannot afford to lose a camper on the very first full day!"

As if we could afford to lose one ever, E.D. thought as she went back downstairs.

Zedediah gathered the campers in the dining tent to give the part of his Opening Ceremony talk he'd originally had to cut, while Cordelia, Hal, Jake, Destiny, and E.D. fanned out over Wit's End to search for Cinnamon. Lucille and Sybil worked on lunch as if everything was completely normal, and Randolph insisted that Archie go back to town to buy walkie-talkies. "If Lucille had had a way to communicate with the rest of the staff, someone could have been sent to get the girl right away!" he said. "This must never happen again!" He had gone to the office, with coffee and a triple-chocolate brownie, "to man the command center," as he said.

E.D., thinking of Cinnamon's threat to go home, had headed into the woods that bordered the county road. The others had started their searches calling the girl's name, but E.D. didn't bother. This was not a kid who'd accidentally gotten lost and would be grateful to be found. It was altogether possible that Cinnamon had set out to hitchhike back to New Jersey. She might even now be riding in the back of some local farmer's pickup truck, heading north.

E.D. kept to the shade of the woods, peering out at the road over the patches of poison ivy and blackberry briars that grew thickly along the shoulder. She wiped the sweat from her face. Even here in the shade the humidity made the air feel almost too thick to breathe. Just ahead the woods ended and the meadow began, separated from the road by an old, sagging, barbed wire fence. It would be much worse to be out there in the direct sun. She stopped for a moment before heading out into the unsheltered meadow. And heard the sound of someone crying.

"Cinnamon?" she called. "What's wrong?"

The sobbing stopped with a gulp and was replaced by loud snuffling, but no answer. E.D. pushed her way gingerly between a blackberry bush and a honeysuckle-draped shrub and found Cinnamon, kneeling on the shoulder of the road, next to the newly dead body of a possum. The girl looked up, her crimson face wet with tears. She wiped her cheeks, leaving streaks of dirt. Her feet, in her blue-sequined flip-flops, were filthy from walking in the dirt at the side of the road. Her cell phone lay on the ground by the corpse. For a moment neither of them spoke.

"Are you okay?" E.D. asked.

"What does it look like? Stupid road," Cinnamon said. "Doesn't anybody ever drive on it?"

E.D. looked at the dead possum. "Somebody did, obviously. Last night, probably. Possums freeze in headlights, you know. What were you doing out here?"

"Looking for some place my stupid phone would work. Or a ride to town. As if!"

"Let's go back. It's nearly time for lunch."

Cinnamon picked up her phone and pushed herself to her feet. "I thought maybe it was just pretending. 'Playing possum,' you know. But it's really, really dead." She wiped her nose with the back of her hand. "Stupid animal. Stupid, stupid, stupid animal!" Then she leaned down and touched its fur, patting it gently, as if it were still alive. "You'd think it could cross a completely deserted road without getting itself killed!"

All the way back to the house, Cinnamon muttered about the stupid road, the stupid possum, and her stupid phone.

Chapter Sixteen

So far, on this first full day, camp was a whole lot like babysitting Destiny, Jake thought as the two of them walked toward the pond in their bathing suits with towels around their necks. Jake was carrying the life jacket Destiny would wear when they went swimming.

"Does all the campers have to go in the water?" Destiny asked.

"Yes. They have to take a swim test before they can have free swim."

"Betcha they won't all! The green twin says she

isn't going in the water ever again. She says the Death Pond tried to pull her in and just about drownded her. She says if you hadn't saved her, she'd be dead now and you're a superhero."

Jake sighed. Ginger had sat next to him at lunch—the only girl at the boys' table—and had given him another poem. She had brought him a handful of Queen Anne's lace. And she stared at him all the time. The girl had become some kind of stalker. "She wasn't *drowning*. She just got stuck in the mud, like Winston does sometimes. The dock's there now, so she won't have to go anywhere near the mud."

"Mommy says the twins are 'dentical. Isn't that s'posed to mean they're just exactly alike?"

"Pretty much. These two are, for sure. If they didn't wear different colors, we couldn't tell which was which."

"That's silly. Except for how they look, they're not the same at all. Cimma—Cim—the blue twin's sad and the green twin isn't. The blue twin's really, really sad."

"Seems to me she's *mad* most of the time."

Destiny shook his head solemnly. "Nope. Sad." He started humming "Twinkle, Twinkle," and stopped suddenly. "Did you know possums gots fingerprints, Jake?"

"What?"

"Fingerprints. Possums got beautiful, star-shaped paws and fingerprints just like us. And beautiful fur, too. The blue twin says they just get a bad rap 'cause of their tails. That's what the blue twin says. She's just like Aunt Lucille about aminals—she talks to 'em."

"What possum? Destiny, what are you talking about?"

"The blue twin and the possum that got killded on the road. She wants to make a funeral for it. She really, really wants to. Can she do that? It would make her feel better."

"How do you know all this?"

"She was crying on the porch of Dogwood Cottage during rest time."

"Where was Cordelia?"

"With everybody else learning walkie-talkies."

"Cinnamon should have been in her room. The campers are supposed to have their feet on their bunks for rest time."

Destiny shook his head. "She didn't want her sister to see her crying. But I saw her. So I went to see what was the matter. The possum was the matter."

Amazing, Jake thought. He would have to tell Lucille about the possum funeral. Maybe Harley, who had so far had only dead bugs to photograph, could take pictures of the deceased. And the funeral too, for that matter.

They had reached the pond now, where the campers, in swimsuits, were all lined up on the dock. Archie was out on the diving platform, a whistle on a lanyard around his neck. Q and David were jostling each other, threatening to throw each other off, while the others did their best to stay out of their way.

Dragonflies buzzed purposefully back and forth across the water, changing direction suddenly, occasionally having what appeared to be a dogfight near the reeds on the far side of the pond. Hal and Cordelia, looking even more stunning than usual in her swimsuit, were stationed on the ramp, cutting off the only route of escape should a camper decide not to participate. Ginger, at the back of the line, had her arms folded across her chest and held her head in an unmistakable attitude of defiance, but clearly the only way she could avoid going into the water would be to jump off the dock sideways and brave the muck.

Archie blew the whistle. "Okay, we'll do this one at a time," he called to them. "Q, you'll dive—or jump—in, swim over here and touch the platform, then swim back to the ladder and climb out. As soon as he's up on the dock, Samantha, you dive in and do the same thing. And so on. When everybody has swum from the dock to the platform and back, we'll have free swim. Got that?"

"When do I gets to go in?" Destiny asked Jake. "I'm hot!"

"Me, too. But not till free swim. You have to put on your life jacket first."

"*They* don't gots life jackets," Destiny said.

"They know how to swim."

"I do too! Paddle and kick. Paddle and kick!"

"Okay, Q," Archie called. "When I whistle, you go."

Q crouched as if for a racing dive, and when Archie blew the whistle again, he launched himself into the water.

"See, Jake? Paddle with your arms and kick with your feet," Destiny said. "I can do that!"

One after the other, the campers dived in, swam to the platform, returned, and took their places at the end of the line until only Ginger was left, standing next to the ladder, her arms still folded. Harley had already climbed out of the water, and the rest of the campers were standing behind her on the dock, waiting to be allowed to go in again. Destiny wasn't the only one who wanted to get into the water.

Archie whistled. Ginger didn't move. "Come ahead," he called.

Jake could feel the sun getting hotter and hotter on his shoulders.

"I wanna swim!" Destiny said. He kicked off his flip-flops and picked up his life jacket. "I *said*, I wanna swim!"

Jake buckled him into his jacket. "Just wait. As soon as Ginger goes, everybody can swim."

"She's not going," Destiny protested. "I told you she wouldn't. You go, Jake. She'll get in if you do, I betcha."

Jake shook his head. "Let Archie handle it."

Destiny suddenly ran toward the dock, pointing into the sky. "Look, look, look!" he shouted at the top of his lungs. While everybody was looking up to where a turkey vulture was circling over the pond, its wings in a steady V, Destiny pushed past Hal and Cordelia and the campers, grabbed Ginger by the arm, and launched himself off the end of the dock, dragging her, shrieking, with him. Jake rushed after him and reached the end of the dock as Ginger and Destiny came up through the cannonball splash, water streaming down their faces. "Paddle and kick!" Destiny hollered as Ginger sputtered and began to tread water. "Paddle and kick! Like me. You can do it!"

And so, of course, she could. While Destiny bobbed cheerfully up and down in his life jacket, smacking the water with both hands and repeating "paddle and kick, paddle and kick," she swam to the platform, touched it, and swam back to the dock.

"I'll get you for this," she said to Destiny as she grabbed hold of the ladder. Then she saw Jake and broke into a smile. She reached up for his hand, so he pulled her up. "Thanks," she said, her face radiant with stalker passion.

Jake groaned.

From the diving platform, Archie's whistle shrilled again. "Free swim!" he called. "When I call 'Buddy check,' grab hands with your buddy and raise them so

I can see!" The campers cheered and flung themselves back into the pond.

"I guess we're buddies," Jake called to Destiny. He held his nose and jumped. The water was wonderfully cool and surprisingly clear. As he came back up, he could see Destiny's feet kicking sporadically beneath the red cylinder of his life jacket. The moment Jake's head broke the surface of the water, Ginger Boniface did a cannonball off the dock that swamped him and Destiny both.

Chapter Seventeen

It was a few minutes after noon on *Eureka!* Day Three, and everyone except Hal (and Randolph, who probably wasn't up yet) had gathered in the dining tent for announcements. E.D. had chosen to sit with Aunt Lucille, Uncle Archie, and her grandfather. As usual the boys and Ginger were at one table and the girls and Destiny, who sat next to Cinnamon, were at another. Watching Q and David, E.D. couldn't help but think of all the nature documentaries where lion cubs or wolf pups or young hyenas were constantly wrestling and chewing on each other. The two of them were at each other every minute.

Obviously, David—however powerful his aura—was *not* an angel. But knowing that did nothing to change the effect he had on her. It was possible it made that effect even stronger. As good as David was at everything, even E.D. was beginning to see that Q was better. She thought about David's application, and how full it was of obvious successes. He was used to being the best. Suddenly, he wasn't. He must feel the way she did last fall when Jake had found the great spangled fritillary—the very last butterfly for her Butterfly Project—the one she'd been looking for for weeks. She'd been furious at him. Hurt and furious!

Jake, as a staff member, ought to at least try to stop the roughhousing, she thought now. But he didn't. In fact, he tended to participate. If somebody punched him, he invariably punched back. What had the family been thinking of to make their resident juvenile delinquent a member of the staff?

Sybil rang the temple gong Lucille had donated for the purpose of getting everyone's attention. She had to do it twice more before it got quiet. "You may be glad to know that from now on all meals will be served buffet style." After several food insurrections, she and Lucille had given up trying to invent menus that would please everybody. "There will be a variety of foods laid out in the kitchen, and you can choose whatever you like—"

"Or whatever you don't hate," David said. David, exercising what leadership he could, had started most of the insurrections.

"In any case," Sybil went on, "your choices will be entirely up to you. As you see on the schedule E.D. gave you this morning, the Required Workshop this afternoon is once again Poetry, which will be held at the pond, because today's subject will be Images of Nature."

"Do we need to bring our journals?" Ginger asked.

"Of course. And something to write with."

David raised his hand.

"Yes? Do you have a question?"

"On Monday Zedediah said individual passion is the source of all creativity."

"Yes—"

"Well, see—I don't have a passion for poetry. I'm pretty good at it, but it definitely isn't a passion."

Q nodded. "It's not exactly my favorite, either. . . ."

"It's *my* passion," Ginger said. "I *love* poetry!"

"I hate it!" Cinnamon said. "It's Ginger's thing. I don't do it, and I'm not *going* to do it!"

Samantha looked up from the fantasy novel she was reading. "If Cinnamon won't, I won't, either. My passion, besides reading, is art. Painting—and sculpture." She went back to her book.

121

E.D. thought of all the hours, all the days, she'd spent figuring out the best way to schedule the workshops. *Nodes of chaos*, E.D. thought. That's what these kids were. *Nodes of chaos!* E.D. loathed chaos.

"I think poetry's actually pretty stupid, if you want to know the truth," David said. "Hardly anybody reads it. And you can't make any money at it!"

Lucille rose from her seat, her face drained of color, a hand at her throat. She looked, E.D. thought, as if someone had suggested using poison on her garden or weed killer in the yard.

"It's nothing against you!" Q said hurriedly. "*Your* poetry's great!"

E.D. waited for David to agree. He didn't. His aura, she thought with a pang, was fading fast.

Instead, David said, "Of all the things I'm good at, it's just singing and dancing and acting that I have a total passion for. You *can* get to be rich and famous doing those things, if you're good enough! I don't think there should *be* required workshops. If you really believe what Zedediah says, we should get to follow our passions."

There was a moment of silence. *Nodes of chaos*, E.D. thought again.

Harley, who had been taking a picture of something on the ground next to his feet and seemed not to have been aware of what the others were saying, looked up then as if the silence had suddenly registered with him. "Instead of poetry," he said in a small and tentative voice, "I'd rather have a workshop in photography, if that would be all right."

Lucille, tears glistening in her eyes, sat back down, and Archie patted her hand comfortingly.

Zedediah stood then. "Let me get this straight," he said. "There is only one camper who wishes to continue focusing on the art of writing poetry, is that correct?"

Everybody nodded.

"It's my most favorite thing in all the world!" Ginger said.

What happened next was something E.D. should have expected the moment Zedediah had first used the word *passion*. She wanted to leap up from her seat and insist on keeping the schedule the way it was. There was such a thing as exploration, as learning. Such a thing as discipline! People ought to be required to do things whether they had a passion for them or not! But she knew she was the only Applewhite who thought that way.

So she sat there, unable to do anything about it, as the whole camp schedule came crashing down around her. Zedediah asked the campers to take some time after lunch to rank the workshops in the order that most interested them. It would be like the lunch buffet, E.D. thought. They would not be required to attend any workshop they didn't want to attend.

Lucille, somewhat recovered, agreed then and there to work with Harley on photography.

"Flexibility," Zedediah said before sending everyone in to get their lunch, "is *also* essential to the creative life!"

All well and good, E.D. thought, but Grandpa didn't have to *schedule* flexibility!

After lunch when the campers had gone off to put their feet on their bunks and create their lists of priorities, E.D., whose Community Service was kitchen cleanup, mentioned to her aunt her thought about the value of exposing the campers to a few things they didn't choose for themselves. "Don't you think that would be good for them?"

Lucille, who had been wiping the counters, straightened up and shook out her cloth. "Nonsense. It would thwart the very essence of who they are. We are not about thwarting essence!"

On her way out of the kitchen, E.D. nearly collided with her father, who had never made it to lunch at all. His hair had not yet been combed, and he looked even more stressed and preoccupied than normal. In one hand he held the usual collection of Applewhite mail: assorted catalogs and advertising circulars, and a few bills. In the other he clutched a crumpled piece of paper.

"What's the matter?" E.D. asked.

"Hmmm? What?" He looked at her abstractedly for

a moment and then made a visible effort to collect himself. "Oh, nothing. Nothing important. Nothing at all."

Right, E.D. thought as she headed for the office. *Nothing.* That was because he hadn't been there to see chaos take over *Eureka!* Whatever was stressing her father, she couldn't think about it now. She had to come up with something to do with five campers this afternoon instead of poetry.

Chapter Eighteen

It was a good thing, Jake thought, that E.D. had been sent out with a folding chair, a lantern, and her walkie-talkie to sit between the boys' bunk and the girls' to listen for possible disturbances so Hal and Cordelia could come to the staff meeting. She'd been freaking all afternoon about the destruction of her precious camp schedule, and the stress level was high enough in the room already. Winston, always upset by intense emotions, had gone from one person to another at first, wagging his tail, trying to comfort everybody. But he'd given up and gone to hide out in the hall. Jake knew how he felt.

So far no one had done anything in this meeting except complain. It hadn't occurred to the family, when they'd planned to have the campers do all the things that gave *them* joy, that the campers were likely to be as different from one another as the Applewhites. The camper priority lists had been something of a shock. Randolph's theater workshop was the only one that all six wanted to take. Jake's singing workshop was next, with five, and then Cordelia's, with four. Even Lucille had lost her usual glow of rosy optimism. "I'd been so looking forward to sharing the joys of poetry with six children. Now there's only one!"

"At least you've got one," Archie said. "Hal and I have to *share* Samantha Peterman."

"The good thing is, that means I only have half a person," Hal pointed out, "or a person only half the time. The bad thing is, she wants to do murals! She says a piece of canvas is too small to hold her vision!"

"It isn't just that I only have one," Lucille said. "It could be wonderful to have only a single budding poet to concentrate on. It could be an opportunity to help shape a whole life's work. But this afternoon I shared with her some of the very best of contemporary American poetry—to show her how magnificent, how transcendent, a poem can be—and she was *impervious*. She listens. She nods. But what does she write? *Verse!*"

Lucille shuddered as she said the word. "All her poems rhyme. They gallop. Da-da-da-da-da-da-da-*dum! Da-da-da-da-da-dum!*"

"It would appear," Zedediah observed, "that she understands rhythm, at least."

Cordelia moaned. "Don't mention that word! While Lucille was doing Poetry, I had Dance. Thanks to all the talk about passion, Q decided the workshop ought to be all about Step! He was like a freight train. He took over entirely. Step. All rhythm. No music. Think about that—dance with *no music!* All foot stomping and hand clapping."

"You have to admit, he's really, really good at it," Hal said.

"Of course he's good at it! He's good at everything! He'd be good at any kind of dance—*including the kind I want to teach!* And then there's David. David brought tap shoes today! I ask you—tap shoes? The two of them were absolutely competing with each other. My workshop has turned into some kind of a reality show. Q teaches the girls a Step routine, so then David insists on getting them to do shuffle, ball, change, which Q does as well as he does, by the way—better, really. I felt like I was caught in a war zone. I couldn't get either of the boys to so much as try a grand jeté or a glissade, and they won't lay a hand on the barre. David called it a crutch! Ginger and Cinnamon have both had ballet, but Cinnamon says she 'prefers modern dance.' What am I going to do? I'd planned that contemporary *Swan Lake* for the end-of-camp show. I'd already started on the choreography!"

Sybil had been curled up in her easy chair chewing on a pencil. Now she spoke. "Cinnamon is the only camper who chose fiction. I talked to her about it at dinnertime, and she tells me Destiny wants her to write a children's book. I have no *idea* how to write a children's book. Plot I can teach. How to slip in clues I can teach. How to create an interesting ongoing character. But Cinnamon wants her main character to be a possum! A *beautiful* possum! She wants it to be a *picture* book so Destiny can do the drawings for it. The absolutely only thing I know about picture books is that they're thirty-two pages long."

"Give Cinnamon some Petunia Granthams to read," Zedediah said. "I should think plot, at least, would be pretty much the same from a Petunia Grantham mystery to a picture book. Except shorter. And without the murder."

Randolph had gotten up and was now pacing around the edge of the room like a tiger in a cage. "Nonessentials!" he said suddenly. "Niggling quibbles! Every one of you is capable of handling a talented kid—even a roomful of them. When you find out what they do best, you just let them do it. Push them a little to do it even more, even better."

Lucille snorted. "I'm a poet! I refuse to encourage Ginger to write *verse*."

Jake had been thinking about the poems Ginger had forced on him. The last few had reminded him a little of country and Western love songs. He raised a tentative hand. "What if you didn't think of her stuff as *poetry*? What if you thought of it as song lyrics? Lyrics pretty much always rhyme."

"Song lyrics." Lucille pondered this for a moment. "Not poetry at all." She nodded. "Pure genius, Jake. Now all we need to do is find somebody she can work with to compose the music! Cordelia? You compose."

"No way," Cordelia said. "I don't do *songs*."

Jake thought about Cordelia's music for her one-woman ballet, *The Death of Ophelia*. All discordant chords and no hint of melody. She had that right!

"What did I tell you?" Randolph said. "Even Jake knows how to do this. Every one of these kids has talent. A good director with talented actors needs to give them their heads, let them experiment, trust them to find their way. The most he does is nudge them in a useful direction. Just be good *directors*. Figure out what they're doing well and support it."

"That should be easy to do with Harley," Lucille said, "if I can get him to take pictures of something besides corpses. He showed me some of his work—he has a fabulous eye for composition and design."

"Workshops aren't problems," Randolph said. "We need to focus on the *problems*!"

"Like what?" Sybil asked.

Randolph turned on Hal and Cordelia. "I looked into the boys' and girls' cottages this afternoon. It looks like tornadoes have been rampaging through there. Clothes, books, papers—*mess*—everywhere! We wouldn't keep the goats in a mess like that."

Cordelia laughed. "If we did, Wolfie would gobble it all up!"

"This isn't funny. This whole place is a disaster. We're only three days in, and already the bathrooms in the cottages are absolutely filthy. The grass is knee-deep—who knows what vermin could be multiplying in there? The green twin claims—"

"Ginger, dear," Sybil put in.

"Whatever! She claims there's a mouse living in their bedroom. And there are ants in the kitchen!"

"I've asked the ants to leave," Lucille said. "They've let me know they're just passing through. They'll be gone by the end of the week."

"Get some ant traps next time you're in town!" Randolph told Archie.

"Don't you dare," Lucille said.

"Nothing at Wit's End is the least bit worse than normal, Randolph," Sybil said testily.

"Normal isn't good enough! This isn't just where we live anymore; it's a camp! A public facility!"

"The kids don't care," Cordelia said. "Well, except Ginger doesn't like mouse pee and poop in her dresser drawers."

"*Well, I care!*"

"Good heavens, why?" Sybil asked.

Zedediah spoke then. "Have E.D. put bathroom cleaning and grass mowing on the Community Service schedule tomorrow. That's not so difficult. Find a live trap for the mouse. Now that I don't have anyone to do workshops for, I'm going back to turning out furniture and making money, you'll all be glad to know. Anybody else have anything worth talking about?"

"I do," Jake said. "I'm a little nervous about my singing workshop. I've got everybody except Harley—"

"That seems very strange, don't you think?" Lucille said. "The son of a pair of singers with a band so successful their concerts are all sold out six months in advance—"

"I think it's just a cult following," Hal put in.

"The point is, his parents are professional singers, and he absolutely refuses to sing."

"Could be that's the reason," Zedediah said. He glanced meaningfully at Archie. "It can be a challenge, competing with a parent."

"Anyway," Jake went on, "Q and David are both great singers, which would be good except that I don't know how to help either one of them get any better. David keeps reminding me that he's had a private, professional coach, and Q has his grandfather, who taught him enough to win all those talent shows. All I did when I taught Destiny to sing was to get him singing with me. I don't have a clue what to do with these guys."

"If you want to learn to play chess," Zedediah said, "the best way is to play with somebody better than you are."

"But isn't a teacher supposed to be better than the people he's teaching? I'm definitely not better!"

Zedediah smoothed his mustache. "This isn't a school. And even if it was, a good teacher is always learning. You're doing a workshop. Think about that word. You're all of you working together. Find out what each of them does best, and make sure everybody else learns from *that*. Make it a collaboration."

"Between David and Q?"

Zedediah laughed. "So think of your job as using their competitive drive to spur them all on to better things. For them, and for you, too. Be as competitive as they are, at least in terms of getting better. Cordelia, same thing. Now, if no one else has anything substantial, I assume we can adjourn. I have a rocking chair order to start on tomorrow."

"Somebody make sure E.D. gets the message about what needs to go on Community Service!" Randolph said. "Hal and Cordelia, it's your responsibility to keep those bunks neat and clean."

"That's why we get the big bucks," Hal said bitterly.

"Very funny. Archie—*ant traps!* And mouse poison. First thing tomorrow!"

Jake saw Archie jump as Lucille pinched his leg. There would be no ant traps or mouse poison, he knew.

"Meeting adjourned!"

Chapter Nineteen

.D. sat alone on the end of the dock, her bare feet in the water, listening to the frogs and katydids calling from all around her. The water felt good. So far she had refused to actually swim in the pond. The idea of living things under and around her that she couldn't see—things that might have teeth or slime or jaws like a snapping turtle—was just too horrible. It was a muggy day as usual, but cloudy, so even though it was late morning, the sun wasn't beating down on her. She kicked her feet, watching the circles the splashes made spread across the surface of the pond.

In spite of the coming of chaos, everybody seemed to be surviving. If anything, Lucille was even happier than usual. With fewer workshops, she had expanded her morning meditation, and the kids actually seemed to be liking it. E.D. suspected some of them were using it to get a little extra sleep—nobody was really doing the lights-out-at-ten thing. But Samantha had told Cordelia that meditation was changing her life. "I used to stress about everything, and now I just breathe!" Yoga, too, had expanded—instead of the sun salutation, it had become a whole forty-minute session. Lucille had flung herself into research on song lyrics and had become practically obsessed about helping Harley to expand his photographic range. "Turns out what he likes about dead things is that they never move, so he can absolutely control the image he gets. We're working on that issue."

Archie and Hal had both come up with projects for Samantha, Cordelia had decided that Step and tap might both be able to be worked into modern dance somehow, and though Jake wasn't talking much about his singing workshop, he'd found a bunch of karaoke music, and Destiny's repertoire had suddenly expanded. Now, whenever he wasn't talking, he was singing. Sybil had decided to learn everything she could about children's books. She'd come back from the library in town with shopping bags full of them and was reading her way through the lot.

Everybody except E.D. herself was loving the theater workshop. She'd joined it as a way to be close to David—even without his aura, the magnet thing was still at work. Cordelia claimed it was hormones and perfectly normal.

The trouble was, Randolph wouldn't let anybody, not even the camp historian, hang out just to observe. E.D. had to do scenes like everybody else. It was easy enough to memorize the words, but she did *not* like having to actually get up onstage and say them. She was painfully aware of how bad she was compared with the other kids. For one thing, she could never figure out what to do with her hands!

Her father knew Jake and the campers loved his workshop. He knew they were doing well, and he could see they were learning stuff all the time. So he should have been as happy as anybody. Instead, he seemed to be getting more and more uptight as the days went by, fussing about things he'd never so much as noticed before, like the time somebody forgot to put the lid on a trash can and a raccoon got into it and strewed trash all over the yard. He'd completely freaked about that—and even picked up some of the mess himself.

And then there was the Fourth of July celebration, when they'd gathered all the campers down by the pond. All the kids were given sparklers, and Archie and Zedediah had set off bottle rockets. Randolph had come tearing down from the house shouting about fireworks being illegal in the state of North Carolina. This had never bothered him before. They'd had fireworks every year since they'd moved to Wit's End, and—

E.D. looked up. Something had moved in her peripheral vision. Something in the woods on the other side of the pond. *Yes.* There it was again. Something—*someone*—was moving among the trees. She reached for the walkie-talkie on her belt and realized she'd left it on the desk back in the office. No, no, no! If this was a camper sneaking away, she'd be in trouble. "Keep these with you at all times," her father had told everyone the day he'd handed them out.

She scrambled up, shoved her feet into her sneakers, and hurried back to shore. As she started around the cattails that lined the edge of the pond toward where she'd seen the movement, a man stepped out of the woods. Instinctively, she crouched down and peered between the reeds. The man was wearing a suit, a white shirt, and a tie, and was carrying a clipboard. He stood for a moment gazing across the pond, jotted something down on the clipboard, and then slipped back among the trees.

He hadn't seen her, apparently. Never once in the whole four years they'd lived here had a stranger turned up on their property, much less a stranger in a suit with a clipboard. *Weird.* Who would go wandering around the countryside dressed like that?

Follow him, a voice in her head told her. *Go tell somebody,* another voice answered. *If you go back to the office now, he'll get away,* the first voice said. *You need to find out what he's doing.* E.D. stood up. The man was no longer visible. She hurried around the pond and ducked in among the trees. Once in the woods, it was hard to move quietly—hard for that matter, with the bushes and vines and fallen branches, to move at all. She stopped to tie her sneakers, and realized that the man was having the same trouble with the underbrush as she was and was making at least as much noise. If she moved slowly and carefully enough, she could follow him by ear without him hearing her.

Five minutes later she realized she had moved *too* slowly and carefully. She couldn't hear him anymore. And of course she couldn't see him. Too many trees, too many vines and bushes. She'd lost him!

Chapter Twenty

A mosquito landed on Jake's arm and he swatted it. He was sitting in his sanctuary atop a vine-shrouded boulder in the woods, having slipped away while Ginger was busy talking to Lucille. It was the only place in the whole of Wit's End that he was safe from her. Nobody knew of this place where he always came when he felt the need to be alone. Not even Destiny had ever found him here. But somebody was very close right now, moving noisily through the woods in his direction. He parted a curtain of leaves and saw

E.D., her back to him, peering anxiously this way and that, apparently looking for something.

"What are you doing?" he asked.

She jumped and spun around. It took her a moment to see him. He should have kept quiet, he realized. She might have gone on past.

"*Shhh*!" she said, and whispered, "Did you see him?"

"See who?" Jake whispered back.

"The man in the suit."

Jake shook his head. "Nobody came by here."

"Rats," E.D. said in her regular voice. "I really did lose him. What are you doing up there?"

Jake sighed. "It's my secret hideaway. At least it *was*."

"Where's Winston?"

"I closed him in my room. I can't bring him out here with me—you never know when he's going to bark at something."

"If he'd been here with you, he would have scared the guy off."

"Yeah, and brought my stalker right to me. She knows that if she finds Winston, she'll probably find me. And she has a free period now."

"Ginger?"

"Of course Ginger. She's like a burr. Or a leech."

"I think it's cute."

"You wouldn't think it was cute if you were the one she was stalking! Lucille's been doing the songwriting workshop in Wisteria Cottage, so Ginger's taken to leaving stuff for me on my bed! Flowers, cookies, songs—all of them dedicated to me—notes on lavender paper. She thinks it's my favorite color because of my room." Jake sighed, and then realized what E.D. had said. *"A man in a suit? In the woods?"*

"Suit and tie! He was skulking around by the pond with a clipboard taking notes. It's weird."

"Yeah. Seriously weird." Jake remembered the black car he and Destiny had seen. "Like that car."

"What car?"

"A plain black car. It started up the driveway one morning. First day of camp, I think it was. Destiny and I thought it was Archie, back from getting groceries in Traybridge, but when we went to see, the guy backed up and drove away. Fast."

"Why didn't you tell anybody?"

"What's to tell?"

"Was he wearing a suit and tie?"

"I didn't get a look at the driver. I barely saw the car before it took off."

E.D. shook her head. "I don't like it. Something's going on, and I want to know what. A guy in a suit skulking around with a clipboard, a car that takes off the moment somebody sees it, and the strange way Dad's been acting."

"What do you mean strange?"

"Like how he reacted to the way Q cut the grass."

Jake laughed. "That was pretty funny. Q after Q after Q all over the place. Kind of like crop circles!"

"Yeah, but that's exactly the kind of stunt Dad should have *admired*. The kind of thing he might have done himself when he was a kid. Instead, he hollered and fussed and made Q cut all the rest so it would look like a plain, ordinary lawn. When did Dad ever care about a lawn? And another thing: he's started going out to the mailbox to collect the mail—*getting up way before noon to do it.*"

That, Jake thought, *was* strange. "Maybe he's expecting a check and wants to be sure nobody else gets it." He stretched and climbed down off his boulder. "Don't tell anybody about my hiding place, okay?"

E.D. looked around her. "Tell anybody? I couldn't find it again if I tried."

"We should go back. It's nearly lunchtime." Jake watched E.D. start back the way she'd come. "Wrong way," he said. He grinned. Could be, he thought, he'd found a crack in E.D.'s organized perfection.

"Right!" she said. "Of course."

Jake led the way back toward the Lodge. Apparently he hadn't lost his sanctuary.

That night Jake sat in the dark barn wondering where E.D. was. She'd never missed a theater workshop before. Maybe she'd finally decided David wasn't worth the humiliation of getting up onstage and going through a scene like some kind of robot. Jake thought it was strange that somebody who could come up with a completely bogus story in two seconds on the phone—like she'd done with Mrs. Montrose when she told her the camp was full—could be so incredibly stiff and awkward onstage speaking memorized lines. It was good that she didn't know the kinds of things David said about her behind her back. If he ever said them to her, Jake intended to deck him.

The stage lights and the houselights had been turned off in the barn. Outside, the sun had fallen below the tree line, but it would still be light for a while yet. Inside, it was hard to make out where Randolph Applewhite was sitting, a slightly darker shadow among the shadows of the rows of empty theater seats.

Randolph's voice came now from the darkness in front of them. "Tonight we're going to play a theater game called Harbor. Half of you will be on one side of the stage and half on the other. I've placed chairs in a line stage left and chairs in a line stage right. Those chairs are docks, and the stage is the harbor. You'll be boats heading from a dock on one side of the harbor to a dock on the other side. The object is to get safely to your new dock without sinking anyone else or getting sunk."

"How will we keep from crashing into each other?" Harley asked.

"That's the whole point of the game. Each of you will decide what sort of boat you are and what sort of noise that boat would make. As you cross the harbor, you'll make your sound so that the other boats will know where you are, and at the same time you have to listen for everybody else."

"Who wins?" David asked.

"Trust him to ask," Q whispered to Jake.

"Nobody *wins*," Randolph said. "This is theater, not sports. Either you all win or you all lose. The successful working of a harbor requires that boats move around without running into one another. The whole point is to get safely to an empty dock on the other side of the harbor. If there's a collision the game starts over again. But—*listen up; this is important!*—no matter how often you have to start over, there is to be *no talking*. No talking during a round, no talking in between. No sounds except the boats. Understood?"

"Understood," they all answered.

"Okay then. Everybody up. No more talking as of *now*."

Jake scrambled to his feet as everybody else was doing, cracking elbows with Q in the process.

Randolph's voice came from the theater seats. It had grown even darker now so that it was no longer possible to see him at all. "Pick a side, find a chair, and sit down. Be thinking about the kind of boat you want to be and what sound it would make. When I say Go, the game will begin."

Jake began moving like a sleepwalker, his hands in

front of him, aware of the sounds of movement around him: of chairs scraping on the stage floor, of grunts and yelps as people bumped into one another. Someone brushed past his hands, but he managed not to run into anyone, and he found a chair by knocking into it. He sat.

"Go!" came the command. Jake stayed sitting for a moment as the others rose around him, beginning to make their boat sounds, before he decided to be a sailboat, making a whispery, blowing sound between his lips meant to be the sound of his hull slipping smoothly through the water. He rose and began moving slowly, straining to see the movement of the others he could feel and hear around him. He was surprised how unsettling it was not to be able to rely on his eyes. And how hard it was to make sense of all the boat noises. Next to him was a puttering engine sound, ahead of him on the other side of the stage a loud foghorn sound of a very large ship. That would be Q. *"Splish, splish, splish"* came from his left—a rowboat maybe? *"Vroooooommm! Vroooooommm!"* ahead and to the right. David. And then, inevitably, Jake thought, the sound of people colliding. Groans rose from all sides of the stage.

"End of round one," Randolph called.

"Don't be so loud," someone said. "I can't hear anybody else."

"Not my fault—"

146

"No talking! Take your places again." A pale light glowed from the seats as Randolph switched on a flashlight briefly. "Not great. That was only forty-five seconds. You've been used to working as individuals. But plays are not just assemblies of individuals. This game is designed to create an *ensemble*. I assume you all know what that means. Theater is a collaborative art. You need to rely on yourselves, of course, but also on one another. When we begin again, remember to listen to the others and assert yourself at the same time. Listen. Share the space. Cooperate. And remember the goal."

The second round lasted very little longer than the first. Jake had been sunk by *Vroooooommm!*, who had been too loud and moving too fast to hear the sound Jake was making or even the *Putt, putt, putt* Jake had been trying to avoid. David had been making so much noise, he must have been expecting everyone just to get out of his way.

In the third round everyone was temporarily blinded by a sudden flash of light. "Everybody freeze!" Randolph shouted. He wouldn't have needed to tell them, Jake thought. They were all dead in the water. Randolph came to the stage with his flashlight and took Harley's camera from him.

"I needed to see where I was!" Harley said. "I was afraid I'd fall off the stage."

"So change docks with somebody at the back. Who's

willing to come to the front?" In the light of the flashlight, Harley and Samantha changed places, and they began again.

Not being able to talk through what had happened in each round, everyone had to figure out for themselves how to do it better. "Can we change what boats we are?" Jake risked asking when he'd been hit again and everyone was stopped. His whispery sound was apparently too hard to hear among all the other boats.

"Do you get to change roles halfway through a play?" Randolph asked.

It took an unbelievable fourteen rounds before they finally found their way to the docks on the opposite sides of the stage without any collisions. Everybody cheered, and Randolph turned the lights back on, which blinded them all over again.

"Remember this!" Randolph said. *"Ensemble!* And just for the heck of it, see if you can get back to your bunks now without your flashlights."

"Will we be doing scenes again tomorrow?" David asked.

"Tomorrow we work with improvisation."

As the campers headed out of the barn, the spotlights that illuminated the barn's parking area were turned out. Jake was always surprised at how dark night in the country was. The light in the windows of the Lodge did little more than show the direction they needed to go. One by one the boat sounds started up around him, though it wasn't really hard to see each other. David's *Vroooooommm!* and Q's foghorn were in front of Jake, the two boys crashing into each other as they went. *Both boats,* Jake thought, *should be at the bottom of the harbor by now.* A moment later Ginger *splish, splish*ed into him.

Chapter Twenty-one

E.D. hurried down the dark hallway, her spiral notebook clutched to her chest, and stood for a moment at the closed door of her parents' bedroom. Before *Eureka!* started they had always left the door open, but her mother insisted on keeping all the bedroom doors closed now in case any campers happened to go upstairs. She didn't want the campers to know that nobody (except E.D. of course) ever made their bed in the Applewhite household. E.D. took a deep breath. With the door closed like this, going into her parents' room felt like spying. *You* are *spying,* she reminded herself. *That's the whole point.* She wanted to find out what was going on with her father. In the Petunia Grantham mysteries, Petunia was always finding critical information by digging through people's trash. There had been nothing useful anywhere else. This was E.D.'s last resort.

She opened the door and slipped inside, shutting it quickly behind her. Her father was in the barn doing the theater workshop. It was the counselors' night off (Cordelia had insisted they get one a week), so she had dragged Hal to town to see a movie. Everybody else was over at Zedediah's watching television. E.D. turned on the overhead light.

There was one wastebasket in her parents' room, and it was nearly full. Perfect. Her father's hysteria about housekeeping had apparently not carried over to his own bedroom. She upended the contents onto the rug. There were plenty of crumpled tissues, a sock with a hole in the toe, some catalogs that should have been put in the recycle box, and several crumpled envelopes and balled-up sheets of white paper. *Petunia Grantham strikes again!* she thought. Gingerly, she fished these out of the pile.

None of the envelopes had been mailed. There were no stamps, no return addresses, not even the address of Wit's End. On each envelope was the name Randolph Applewhite, spelled out in letters that had been cut from magazines or newspapers and pasted in place, like ransom notes from a kidnapper. It gave the envelopes a threatening air.

She smoothed out one and slipped it into her spiral notebook. The others she put back with the rest of the trash. Then she picked up one of the balled-up sheets of paper and carefully straightened it out. It had been printed on what looked like an ink-jet printer. There was not much on it, but what there was sent a shiver up her spine.

15A NCAC 18A.1004 PERMITS

No person shall operate a summer camp within the State of North Carolina who does not possess a valid permit from the Department.

It had to have been copied from an official document. Department of what? She thought back to the months of preparation for *Eureka!*, trying to remember whether anyone had ever mentioned having to have a permit or having to deal with the state.

Hurriedly, she opened another crumpled sheet.

15A NCAC 18A.1001 DEFINITIONS

"Summer Camp" includes those camp establishments which provide food or lodging accommodations for groups of children or adults engaged in organized recreational or educational programs.

She wondered how many children constituted a group.

> "Department" shall mean the Secretary of the Department of Environment and Natural Resources or his authorized representative. "Sanitarian" shall mean a person authorized to represent the Department on the local or state level in making inspections pursuant to state laws and regulations.

State laws and regulations. What kinds of laws and regulations? She pulled open another wad of paper.

> 15A NCAC 18A.1005 PUBLIC DISPLAY OF GRADE CARD
>
> Inspections of summer camps shall be made in accordance with this Section at least once during each season's operation. Upon completion of an inspection, the sanitarian shall remove the existing grade card, issue a grade card, and post the new grade card in a conspicuous place where it may be readily observed by the public upon entering the facility.

There was no official grade card posted where it could be observed by the public—or anywhere else. She spread the last page out on top of the others.

15A NCAC 18A.1008 GRADING

The sanitation grading of all summer camps shall be based on a system of scoring wherein all summer camps receiving a score of at least 90 percent shall be awarded Grade A; all summer camps receiving a score of at least 80 percent and less than 90 percent shall be awarded Grade B; all summer camps receiving a score of at least 70 percent and less than 80 percent shall be awarded Grade C; and no summer camp receiving a score of less than 70 percent, or Grade C, shall operate.

Official language was stupidly repetitious and obvious, E.D. thought. Were they writing for five-year-olds? But then she looked again at the last part. Without a grade of at least C, *no summer camp shall operate.* Did that mean the state could shut them down?

Were these messages warnings or threats? *Threats.* Why else the cut-and-pasted letters on the envelope? And why was her father keeping these messages a secret? He was engaging in a classic cover-up, E.D. thought with a sinking feeling in her stomach. She had once done a research paper on political cover-ups. She knew where they led. Nowhere good.

She also knew it was illegal to put anything other than actual mail into somebody's mailbox. So whoever was doing it must be waiting till after the mail had been delivered. Who could it be?

E.D. flashed, suddenly, on the first morning of camp. The phone call from Mrs. Montrose about the rejection of Priscilla. "Tell your father he hasn't heard the last of this." These messages were exactly the sort of thing Mrs. Montrose would do. But was she just threatening, or had she actually turned them in to the state?

The man in the suit. The plain black car Jake had seen. Mrs. Montrose *must* have turned them in. They were being watched by "the department"!

E.D. folded the smoothed-out pages and put them in her spiral notebook. She gathered up the rest of the trash and put it back in the wastebasket. She knew something nobody else except her father knew. Something he didn't want the rest of the family to know. The question was, What should she do about it?

Chapter Twenty-two

Staff meetings had gotten very short and less full of complaint. Except for Randolph. He was on a rampage now about food storage, going on and on about whether eggs and milk were being kept at sufficiently low temperatures to prevent spoilage. And whether the lunch buffet allowed tuna or chicken or egg salad to be at room temperature long enough to risk salmonella or botulism.

"Has any one of us ever gotten salmonella or botulism?" Lucille asked when Randolph took a breath. She didn't need to wait for an answer. "Well, there you are. We are actually feeding the campers considerably better and more carefully than we have ever fed the family!"

"Give us a peanut!" Paulie screamed from his perch, then burst into hysterical laughter.

It really was uncanny, Jake thought, how often Paulie managed to connect with what was being said.

"Let's get on with it," Zedediah said. "Anybody have anything important to report?"

Hal nodded. "Samantha's planning to do her mural on the side of the barn! The barn needs painting anyway. She wants to do all nature images—with maybe a few elves or fairies."

"And we have our first interworkshop cross-fertilization," Lucille said. "Harley's started taking pictures of things that aren't dead: leaves, flowers, the pond. As long as they don't move. He's taking pictures to give Samantha some ideas. He'll make a photo-montage, and she'll paint a version of it on the side of the barn. She wants it to be like a gigantic patchwork quilt, end-to-end and ground-to-roof."

Randolph began muttering about the danger of allowing a camper on a ladder.

"We're putting up a scaffold," Archie said.

"I have news as well!" Sybil said. She looked around the room, beaming with satisfaction. "*I have begun a new book.*"

"Raising Petunia Grantham from the dead, are you?" Archie asked.

"Not quite. I've begun writing a children's book. The heroine is Petunia Possum."

"Isn't that the name of Cinnamon's picture book?" Randolph asked. "Do you mean you're *plagiarizing* a camper?"

"It isn't plagiarism. It's cross-fertilization. I thought about what Zedediah said about working together. So Cinnamon and I have created a character. She's putting the character into a picture book with illustrations by Destiny; I'm putting her into a mystery book for older children. Cinnamon's been hanging around the goat pen to get to know Wolfie. He's going to be her villain."

"Isn't it beneath you to write a children's book?" Randolph said.

"I've been doing research. The main difference between literature for children and literature for adults is the age—or in this case the species—of the protagonist. With a bit of luck—you know perfectly well I've always had uncommonly good luck—children's books can make a *fortune*. Consider Harry Potter. An absolute fortune!"

At that moment Hal's walkie-talkie chirped. "Mayday, Mayday," E.D.'s voice called. "Q and David are throwing each others' clothes out the window of the cottage."

Hal went pale. "I can't," he said. "I can barely deal with them when they *aren't* fighting."

"I'll go," Zedediah said, holding his hand out for Hal's walkie-talkie. "On my way," he said into it. He turned back at the door. "Meeting's over anyway, right?"

Randolph nodded abstractedly. "A fortune," he muttered as everyone else in the room stood up to leave. "An absolute fortune. . . ."

Jake sat on a log at the fire circle where E.D. had brought him when she'd materialized out of the darkness as he and Winston left the staff meeting. Lightning bugs were blinking on and off around them. She was sitting next to him, the messages she had found in her father's wastebasket spread on the ground in the light from her flashlight. "I'm going to watch the mailbox and see who's leaving these things. But it may be too late. Remember how upset Mrs. Montrose was when we rejected Priscilla? I'm pretty sure she's behind this. Bet you anything she's already reported us to the state."

Jake nodded. "It's just the kind of thing that woman would do." Winston whuffed at a firefly. "You think the state could shut *Eureka!* down?"

"Looks like it! And if we get shut down, the families won't have to pay for the rest of camp. We'll lose Wit's End! I keep thinking about that hovel in New Jersey."

"Your mother says she's about to make a fortune writing a children's book, and Zedediah's working—"

"It's a lot more than the money now, though. Everybody's gotten committed to *Eureka!* If the state shuts the camp down it will be a *failure*. A massive—*public*—failure! Do you have any idea what it would be like for the whole family to fail at something? All at once? Bad enough if one single person gets a negative review. You should have been here the time the Petunia Grantham mysteries were called 'literary potato chips' in the *New York Times*! Or when some stuffy art critic said Uncle Archie's Furniture of the Absurd was not only absurd but 'ill-conceived and badly executed.' Notice that I can quote these things! Ask any one of them if they've ever had bad press, and they'll be able to repeat word for word every negative thing anybody ever said about them! Applewhites do not handle failure well. To have *Eureka!* shut down would be—would be—I'm not sure we'd ever recover."

Jake sighed. "I get it."

"The point is, *What are we going to do?*"

Jake shrugged. "What *can* we do? And how come your father's keeping all this a secret?"

"That's easy. *Eureka!* was his idea. If it fails, he'll get all the blame. Uncle Archie and Grandpa will take him apart for not going to the state in the first place. At least it explains why he's been so obsessed about stuff like mice and garbage. I was beginning to fear for his sanity."

"Does he know about the guy in the suit?"

"I don't think so."

"You should tell him. Maybe he could just call the department of whatever it is and ask what he needs to do to make everything legal."

"This is Randolph Applewhite we're talking about. The director. Directors think they rule the world. My father doesn't knuckle under. *Rules are made to be broken*. That's practically a family slogan."

Somewhere in the woods an owl hooted—twice, then twice more. "In that case we need to take it to the whole family," Jake said. "We did a theater game about the power of ensemble—where everybody wins or everybody loses. If it works for these kids, it'll work for anybody. *All for one and one for all!*"

Chapter Twenty-three

It was 9:43 A.M. and E.D was crouched in the bushes between the house and the road, watching the mailbox. Almost always the mail was in their box by ten, and it wasn't there yet. A seriously annoying sharp twig was sticking her in the back of the neck, and occasionally one of the big, black ants that were charging purposefully around among the leaves would get sidetracked and end up crawling up her arm or—worse—down her shirt. So far none of them had bitten her at least.

She had peeked in on her father before she came

outside. He'd been asleep, tangled in the sheet as if he'd been fighting to free himself from some dream monster. An alarm clock, an item seldom used in the Applewhite family by anybody except E.D., had been standing on his bedside table, close to his head. That was how he'd been getting up in time to be at the mailbox by about ten thirty—the crack of dawn in his world. She had crept in and turned off the alarm.

As she was brushing away another ant, she heard an approaching vehicle. She peered between the leaves. It was the mail truck, coming fast down the empty road and angling toward their mailbox. It pulled to a stop with a screech of brakes, its hazard lights blinking. An arm reached out and opened the box. The arm withdrew into the truck, then reappeared with a batch of mail, flung it into the very back of the mailbox, and slammed the door shut. With a squeal of tires on hot pavement, the truck headed on down the road.

E.D. waited. Nothing. Nothing. She watched the heat waves wrinkling the air above the empty road. An ant began crawling up her bare leg. She stomped her foot to dislodge it. A yellow jacket buzzed past her head. A crow called from the field across the road. If this was what it was like to be a detective on stakeout, Petunia Grantham could have it! Jake had a workshop this morning or she'd have taken him up on his offer to do the stakeout. She was glad it was all happening *after Jake* instead of before, she thought. It meant she had an ally. Now, instead of driving her crazy, his combination of creativity and good sense was a comfort.

Finally, she heard the sound of a distant car coming from the direction the mail truck had gone. It was a black car. A plain black compact car.

The car veered out of its lane and across the road, heading toward the mailbox directly into what would have been oncoming traffic, if there had been any, which, of course, there was not. As the car slowed, the window went down. A bare, hairy arm reached out, slipped an envelope into the mailbox, and disappeared again. The window went up as the car lurched forward, veered back into its own lane, and sped away.

E.D. waited another long minute and then hurried to the mailbox. The envelope looked just like the others—RANDOLPH APPLEWHITE was spelled out in pasted-on letters. She ripped it open and pulled out the page inside.

15A NCAC 18A.1012 RECREATIONAL WATERS
A natural or artificial body of water may be approved by the Department for recreational purposes based upon the results of inspections, bacteriological examinations of the water, and sanitary surveys.

She stuffed the page and envelope into her pocket and headed for the dance studio, where Jake would be preparing for his singing workshop.

When she got there, Winston, who had been asleep on an old beach towel in the corner, came wagging over to greet her. She reached down to rub his ears. Jake was setting out the folding chairs for his workshop. "Another message came," she told him.

"Did you see who brought it?"

"Only his arm. But it was the car you saw the first day of camp. Plain and black." She gave him the sheet of paper and waited while he read it.

"*May* be approved? So they could refuse to approve the pond for swimming." Jake shook his head. "Do you suppose that guy took some water for testing?"

"He'd have had to step in the muck to get close enough to collect a sample."

"He could've gone out on the dock to get it."

"I was on the dock when he showed up at the pond. He came from the woods on the other side. All he did was look at it for a while and take some notes. We should tell everybody tonight at the staff meeting."

Jake shook his head. "If we tell them all at once, they'll gang up on your father."

Jake was right, of course.

"And once they gang up, he'll naturally have to fight back. Hard to get an ensemble going after that."

"So what do we do instead?"

"Tell them one at a time. Ask everybody just to think about it for a while and not to talk to anybody else. In that harbor game everybody had to keep quiet. It keeps people from arguing, and that makes them have to think."

"I saw Aunt Lucille and Harley over by the woodshop as I was coming here," E.D. said. "I think it would be good to tell her first."

"Okay. And I could tell Archie after my workshop. We'll just tell them not to talk about it yet."

When E.D. got to the woodshop, Lucille and Harley were outside taking pictures of what looked like a huge tangle of honeysuckle and wisteria vines stretched between two upright branches maybe four feet tall that were set into buckets of sand. The sweet smell of the honeysuckle blossoms filled the air. They didn't notice E.D. at first.

"Don't focus too long or too hard," Lucille was telling Harley. "Just keep clicking and changing your angle the tiniest bit each time. You never know what angle of light or what perspective will make the difference between a snapshot and a work of photographic art. The more images you get, the better your chances."

"But I want to know ahead of time exactly what I'm getting," Harley said. "I want to control how it turns out. . . ."

"I know. But you need to leave room for the magic," Lucille said. "Craft is about control. Art requires magic."

"Excuse me," E.D. said, "but can I talk to you for a minute, Aunt Lucille? In private?"

Harley clicked his camera shutter, moved a little, and clicked again.

"Sure," Lucille said. "What do you think of Samantha's sculpture? It's her first project for Archie's workshop. She calls it an Elf Net."

E.D. seldom understood Uncle Archie's work, but the Elf Net was pretty. And interesting. She could almost imagine elves making it—to catch birds maybe, or unwary people tramping around in their world. "But won't the honeysuckle blossoms die?"

"That's why Samantha wants me to take pictures of it now," Harley said. "She thinks that way it can be two different pieces of art. One when the net's alive and one when it's just a skeleton."

"That ought to be right up your alley," E.D. said.

"The live one won't last," Lucille said, "but the pictures will. There will still be a three-dimensional sculpture after the vines die, but Harley's work captures and keeps images of the original."

"Dead things don't seem quite so dead," Harley said, "when you've still got pictures of them."

"You keep working here," Lucille told Harley. "Go on changing perspectives. I'll just talk to E.D. for a minute or two." E.D. and Lucille moved around to the other side of the woodshop. "What's up?" Lucille asked.

E.D. explained about the messages in the mailbox.

"Just like Randolph to keep it a secret," Lucille said. "Archie'll never let him hear the last of this."

"That's why Jake thinks it would be better for everybody just to think about it for a while before we get together—maybe there doesn't have to be a fight. Dad doesn't even know all of it." E.D. told Lucille about the man in the suit.

"You think he's a state inspector?" Lucille asked.

"What else? If we don't pass inspection, they'll close us down."

"There must be something we can do."

Harley's voice startled both of them. "Distract and delay."

E.D. and Lucille turned. He had come around the woodshop and heard at least the last part of the conversation.

"What do you mean?" Lucille asked him.

"It's the state you're talking about, right?" Harley asked. "That means bureaucracy and red tape. Nothing ever works fast. If the guy's an inspector, he has to finish the inspection and make his report before anybody can do *anything*. And it's never just one person who can make a decision. One guy has to call another, and that guy has to get somebody else

168

to sign something. It can take just about forever."

"How do you know this?" Lucille asked.

Harley shrugged. "My parents deal with bureaucrats all the time when they're setting up their concerts. Permits for this, permits for that. They say the best way to handle any problem you have with a bureaucracy is *distraction and delay.*"

Chapter Twenty-four

"Are we going to do some *solo* work today, O Great Emperor of Singing?" David said as he came into the dance studio. "I don't see how all this 'sing-along' stuff is worth my time. It's not like I'm planning to join a *chorus*."

Jake turned from the table where the music system was set up. Q had come in behind David and was heading for a chair. "Q? You have any thoughts about that?"

"Sure! One, harmony. Can't learn harmony by

singing alone all the time. Two, you ever been in a musical?"

David sniffed. "Sure. We did *Guys and Dolls* at school last year."

"Then you've already sung with a chorus! Musicals are ensembles just like the rest of theater. You can't just be like those dudes on television, showing off their style all the time."

David turned a chair around and straddled it. "Nothing wrong with the 'dudes on television'! My vocal coach says—"

Jake broke in. "We can do solos today if everybody wants to."

Samantha had come in and taken a seat. "I do a terrific 'Over the Rainbow.' Do we have the music for it?"

Cinnamon stuck her head in the door. "Anybody know where Destiny is? He usually meets me at the dining tent, but he wasn't there."

"Last I saw him was breakfast," Q said.

"He was with your sister after yoga," David said.

"*She's* not here either!" Jake realized he ought to have noticed this a whole lot sooner. Ginger was always the first person to show up for his workshop. Most of the time she brought him a present of some kind. Or a snack for Winston.

Jake picked up his walkie-talkie. "Anybody know where Destiny is? Or Ginger?"

After a moment Cordelia responded. "Not in Dogwood Cottage."

"Not in the art studio," Hal answered.

"They're not by the woodshop, either," E.D. reported.

"Better send a search party," Archie said through a crackle of static.

Jake had just begun to consider whether he should go ahead with the workshop and let the rest of the staff look for Ginger and Destiny when he heard Destiny's voice in the distance. He was singing a song he'd learned at the last workshop when they were doing the music from *West Side Story*. After a moment Ginger's voice joined in, both of them singing at the top of their lungs about how pretty they felt as they came steadily closer.

"Ta-dah!" Ginger said as she came bursting in through the door. In one hand she carried her canvas bag. In the other she held Lucille's hair clippers, which she waved triumphantly in the air. Both sides of her head were shaved, a little patchily, all the way to the scalp. Down the center of her skull ran a raggedy-looking strip of carroty frizz.

Destiny followed her in and Jake groaned. Now, for sure, he thought, Sybil was going to kill him. All that was left of Destiny's thick white-blond hair was a narrow stripe of buzz cut. "My Mohawk gotted a little short," he said. "Ginger's hand slipped. But she says it's okay cuz it'll grow right back."

Chapter Twenty-five

The good thing about Destiny and Ginger having new and grotesquely bad haircuts, E.D. thought, was that it distracted her family from the power of the government of North Carolina to swoop in and destroy their lives. Everybody knew about it now, but as far as she knew, nobody had started in on her father yet.

She had come into the camp office thinking of going online to see if she could check whether the warning messages were official state regulations or counterfeits. It had come to her suddenly that Mrs.

Montrose might have invented the whole thing just to freak out the man who had traumatized her daughter. There might be no such department and no such rules. But Harley was already at the computer when she came in, uploading the photographs from his camera. Even now they were flashing on the screen for a split second, one after another.

She would figure out tomorrow's schedule instead and get online later. She settled at the desk and spread copies of the previous day's schedules out so that she could see who had done which Community Service chores. She could just imagine the cry that would go up if she accidentally assigned anyone to bathroom cleaning two days in a row. It was bad enough when Q noticed that David had not yet had to clean bathrooms a single time. Nobody had bought her protest that it had been an oversight. She would give David the job tomorrow and prove that she hadn't been playing favorites.

"No!" Harley said now from the computer. *"No!"*

"What?" she asked.

"There's something wrong with this computer."

"It's old!" she said. She was used to the machine's sudden fits and sulks. She got up and went over to see if there was anything she could do. "Is the cursor being slow again?"

The photo on the screen was one Harley must have taken in the theater workshop she'd missed.

The campers were scattered around the stage in various awkward poses.

"Look! Just look! Right above their heads."

E.D. looked more closely. In the air above the campers' heads she could see four perfectly circular splotches of different sizes and slightly different colors. Like pale balls of colored light. "What are those?" she asked.

"I don't know what they are. I've never seen anything like them. There must be something wrong with the computer."

She touched one on the screen. Nothing.

"They aren't on the monitor," Harley said, "they're *in the picture*!"

"Maybe they're waterdrops. Could some water have gotten into your camera somehow? Or onto the lens?"

"No way."

"What happens if you zoom in on them?"

Harley zoomed in on the largest splotch. There was a kind of pattern in the middle of it, like one of Aunt Lucille's meditation mandalas. It had a bluish fringe around the edge that reminded E.D. of the way children draw points around the sun to show that it's shining. Whatever this was, it was a part of the photo, all right. The more he zoomed in, the fuzzier and more pixilated it got, but there was no way to tell what it was. He zoomed in on the others, one at a time. The two smaller ones were just plain white and hazy, with no patterns in the middle; both of the larger ones—a pinkish one and one with a tinge of gold—had the mandalas and the bluish fringe. They were quite pretty really.

"It *could* be the camera," she said. "A light leak or something."

Harley shook his head. "I've been taking pictures with this camera for a year, and I haven't ever had this happen before."

"Did you notice it on the camera screen right after you took the picture?"

Harley shook his head again. "The screen's too small to see something like this. Anyway, it was dark. That's why I took it in the first place. I wasn't even trying to take a picture; I just needed the light from the flash."

"Check out the other pictures."

He closed that photo and clicked on another of the thumbnails on the screen. This one was a dead dragonfly caught in a spiderweb. It had been taken on the front porch of the Lodge. There were no splotches in this picture.

"There," Harley said. "I told you it wasn't the camera."

"It isn't the computer, either, then. Try another."

Harley clicked on another thumbnail. "No! No, no, no!" he said as the photo filled the screen.

This was one of the photos he'd taken of Samantha's Elf Net. It took E.D. a minute to see what he was pointing at. A large bluish-pinkish sphere seemed to be floating a little above it, faint against the silvery siding of the woodshop. It was considerably bigger than the ones in the other picture.

"That wasn't there when I took the picture!"

He clicked then on the photo he'd taken in the dining tent at lunch when everybody was going ballistic over Destiny's and Ginger's hair. Destiny and Ginger were standing together, grinning into the camera. There were clusters of balls of light around their heads—all with mandala centers. There were also two misty white ones down near Ginger's green-sequined flip-flops and a small, very bright thing that was more of a cylinder than a ball. It looked as if it had been caught moving—a line of white stretched out behind a bright circle in the front.

"I gather you didn't see anything like those when you took that picture, either."

"You were there! There was *nothing*!"

E.D. found herself literally scratching her head. "Did you take them all with a flash?"

Harley shrugged. "The first one. And this one. I guess the Elf Net one could be one I used the flash for. Lucille wanted me to try different kinds of lighting."

"So maybe the flash lit up dust particles in the air.

You know how you can see dust in the air when sunlight comes through a window? Dust you can't see otherwise?"

Harley pointed at the one that seemed to be moving. "How fast can a speck of dust move? Do you have any idea how fast dust would have to be going to make that long a streak in the split second of a flash?"

"Pretty fast."

"Yeah. Pretty darn fast!"

"Aunt Lucille ought to see this," E.D. said. She unclipped her walkie-talkie and called her. "Can you come to the office?"

"Tell her 9-1-1," Harley said.

"It isn't an emergency," E.D. said. "The photos aren't going anywhere." He pointed at the screen where he had called up the second photo he'd taken in the dining tent at lunch. The picture was filled with balls of light. It looked like a swarm, all sizes and intensities, so thick they almost obliterated the images of Destiny and Ginger. *What were those things?*

"9-1-1!" Harley repeated.

"9-1-1!" E.D. added. "Lucille to the office, please, 9-1-1." She looked at the last photo again. "The dining tent could be very dusty," she said. But these balls of light just didn't look like dust. And if they were, how come they weren't in the picture he'd taken in the same place just a moment before?

By the time Lucille arrived, pink and breathless, a first aid kit in her hand, with Archie and Zedediah behind her, Harley had the theater workshop photo on the screen again.

"Who's hurt?" she asked.

Harley didn't answer. He just pointed to the balls of light in the photo.

"Ooooooh, Harley!" Lucille exclaimed, dropping the first aid kit on the floor and hurrying to peer at the computer screen. "Orbs! You've caught *orbs*! I've never had them. Not once!"

"What are orbs?" Harley asked.

"Dust," Zedediah said. "An optical anomaly. The barn's a dusty place."

"So says the skeptic," Lucille said. "Nobody knows for sure. I've got a book about orbs, and I think the author's right. I think they're spirits. *Friendly spirits!*"

"Dust particles," Zedediah said. "Causing a flare in the flash."

"Could be water molecules," Archie said. "Humid as it is here, it could be water molecules catching the flash."

"For artists, the two of you are sadly lacking in imagination. I think they're *conscious beings from other dimensions*. Like the nature spirits that help me garden." Lucille smiled hugely. "I love that they've showed up at *Eureka!* The book's author says they're drawn to light and joy. It means we're doing something right! Are there any in your other photos?"

Harley began showing the other pictures, and E.D. decided to take the schedules up to her room and work on them there. She was not fond of things she couldn't understand. Even less fond of things nobody could understand.

Chapter Twenty-six

BRINGING LIGHT

I long to go out fishing
On a midnight sea of stars,
To net one constellation
And catch the fire of Mars.
I'd bring them gently back to Earth
And offer them to you
To chase the shadows from your heart
Whenever you are blue—
To chase the shadows from your heart

And light your world anew.

You'd feel their crystal brilliance
And know that they were there
Forever when the nights seemed dark
And your heart was full of care.

Forever when the nights grow dark
May you remember me
And feel the light I wished to bring
From a far-off midnight sea.

Your BFF, Ginger

Jake, on his way to the theater workshop, read the page he'd found stuck into his camp bag after dinner. And read it again.

"What are you reading?" Harley, with two cameras around his neck instead of one, had come up behind him.

"Something Ginger wrote."

"Pretty radical, that girl! Can you imagine what her parents'll say when she gets home without hair? Is that the lyrics for another song?"

Jake nodded. "Working with Lucille is really making a difference."

Harley laughed. "In more ways than one. She says she found the hair clippers in the bathroom at

Wisteria when she was there for Poetry and smuggled them out in her bag. Can I see what she wrote?"

Jake gave the page to Harley, who read it as they walked. When he'd finished reading, Harley stopped. Jake went on a few steps and then looked back. Harley was staring off into the middle distance. "What?" Harley didn't answer. He didn't even seem to have heard. "Earth to Harley, Earth to Harley!"

Harley shook himself a bit, as if he really had come back from some other place. "This is weird. I'm hearing music in my head."

"Like when you get a song stuck in your mind?"

"No. Nothing I ever heard before." He read the page again. *"I think it's the tune for Ginger's song.* Like it was just there in my head waiting for the words. Wow! Would it be okay if I kept this for a while?"

Jake shrugged. "I don't see why not. She's been wanting to find a composer. Maybe you're it."

Footsteps came thundering down the path behind them, and David pushed his way between them. "He's what? What's this?" He snatched the paper from Harley's hand.

Jake snatched it back. "None of your business."

"Touchy, touchy!" David looked at Harley. "How come the extra camera?"

Harley shrugged. "It's an experiment. Lucille wants me to take pictures of the workshop tonight with both cameras to see which one works better."

"Photographing people now, huh? What'd you do, run out of corpses?"

David went on ahead, and Jake gave Ginger's lyrics back to Harley. "Everybody's favorite camper," he said when he thought David was out of earshot.

"And God's gift to the theater," Harley said.

"Yeah, well, we'll see how he does with improv," Jake said. "He won't have anybody else's words to rely on."

Harley folded the paper and slipped it into his pocket. "Improv's sorta scary."

Q joined them. "It's my favorite thing of all! Except dancing."

Inside, Randolph told them to find seats. But there were only five chairs on the stage. Cinnamon and Ginger got there first, Samantha and E.D. joined them, and David and Q had a brief shoving match to see who would get the last chair. David won and stuck his foot out to trip Q. Q jumped nimbly over it.

"The people in the chairs will do the first exercise," Randolph said. "Jake, Q, and Harley, come sit down here in the house."

"Lucille asked me to take some pictures," Harley said. "Would that be okay?"

Randolph thought for a moment. "We'll make it part of the exercise. Okay, listen up! This is improvisation. That means you invent it all—words, actions, interactions—as you go along. We'll do an exercise about *emotion*. The setup is a party. Samantha, you'll be the host. The others will be the guests. Here's how it works. The stage is your living room, and wherever you choose to see it, there's a front door. The doorbell rings—I'll say *ding dong*—and you go to answer it. Whoever is at the door comes in expressing an emotion as vividly as possible."

"Do you want us to talk?" David asked.

"Sometimes words help, sometimes they don't—it's up to you. So the first person—that'll be you, Cinnamon—comes in with an emotion; and Samantha, as the host, you need to pick up the emotion, whatever it is. The two of you will then create a scene using that emotion. Then the doorbell will ring again and a second guest—that'll be you, Ginger—will come in. You also come in expressing a vivid emotion, but a different one. The other two 'catch it' from you, and you all create a scene with this second emotion. The doorbell rings, and so it goes. Each new person brings a new emotion, and the others pick it up and run with it. After Ginger it's David, after David it's E.D. Got that?"

Everyone on the chairs nodded. "Now one more twist," Randolph said. "Harley, you'll take some pictures during the party; and when the flash goes, everybody will revert to the previous emotion until the next flash. So—let's say there's been anger and then grief. When the flash goes, whoever's at the party has to go immediately from grief back to anger. Give them a little time with that, Harley, then take another picture. At that flash, everybody goes back to grief. Don't take too many, Harley, and don't take them too fast. Give the scenes a chance to develop before you switch them."

Jake was glad he wasn't in the first group. It was fun watching. When the doorbell rang and Samantha opened the imaginary door, Cinnamon stormed in, swearing like Paulie about some fool who'd cut her off in traffic.

It took Samantha a moment to catch the emotion, but then she yelled, "That creep! I hate when that happens! Some fool did that to me just the other day, and I crashed right into his bumper."

"Serves him right!" Cinnamon said. "And I was going to bring a cake for the party, but the stupid bakery got the order wrong. . . ." The two girls ranted on till Randolph interrupted with *"Ding dong."*

Ginger came in laughing. She said nothing, just laughed steadily harder till she was nearly hysterical. Jake found himself chuckling even though she hadn't explained what she was laughing about. She never did use words—just kept on laughing until the others were laughing with her. By then the laughter was real. Everybody—both onstage and off—was laughing when Harley's flash went off. Ginger immediately stopped laughing and shouted at Harley for taking a picture when she wasn't ready. The others joined in, Cinnamon once more cursing like Paulie on a roll.

David brought fear in with him, claiming to be running from a clutch of zombies. That gave everybody a chance to scream and shriek and run around.

When it was E.D.'s turn, though, she came in looking as if she'd just lost her last friend in the world. "My dog!" she wailed. "Someone just ran over my dog! I got him as a puppy from the pound. The poor little thing had been beaten half to death. He was so little and so scared he couldn't even eat. I had to feed him by hand, a bite at a time. That was five years ago, and he's been with me practically every minute ever since. He slept on my feet every night. And now he's gone! He's gone! What'll I do?"

Amazing, Jake thought. What had happened to E.D. the robot? He had a sudden, horrible image of Winston lying in the road. It was as if a sharp stone were lodged in his throat as he thought of Winston never again throwing himself onto his chest as he lay in bed.

Cinnamon had actually started to cry now. "Just like the possum," she choked out the words. "The beautiful possum, dead in the road! Murdered!"

Harley's timing was perfect, Jake thought. Just as Cinnamon hollered *murdered,* he took a picture and everyone had to go back to fear.

⊙⊙⊙

After the workshop, as they all headed back to the cottages, David kept shouting about the zombies coming out of the woods till everybody was screaming and running from the imaginary horrors chasing them. Archie came out with a flashlight to see what catastrophe was going on, and Lucille and Sybil decreed there should be a campfire with s'mores to get them focused on something cheerier before bedtime. As the campers went to find sticks for toasting marshmallows, there were several more zombie scares and at least two sightings of vampires. It was amazing, Jake thought, how scary running in the dark could be. The more you ran, especially if someone was screaming nearby, the more certain you were that something was chasing you. At one point E.D. jumped out at him from behind a tree brandishing a marshmallow stick, and he practically jumped out of his skin.

"Scared you!"

"Startled me is all," he said.

Q appeared and pointed over Jake's shoulder with a look of horror on his face. *"Aaaaah!"* he screamed.

When both Jake and E.D. turned to look, Q yelled "Gotcha!" and ran off.

"That improv thing was really fun, wasn't it?" E.D. said.

Jake nodded. "And you think you aren't creative!"

E.D. shrugged. "Maybe I'm just a really good liar!"

"Maybe that's one definition of creative."

"Jake, Jake!" Ginger came running up with two marshmallow sticks. She gave him one of them, and E.D. went off to get a marshmallow. "Did you read my new lyrics yet? Did you? Did you?"

"I did. I think they're really good. And guess what— Harley thinks he has the music for them. Could be he's the composer you're looking for."

Ginger ran a hand through her raggedy Mohawk. "Lyrics by Ginger Boniface, music by Harley Schobert?"

"Sounds good to me."

"Maybe his parents would record it!" She handed him the other marshmallow stick. "Where is he?"

"Out there somewhere chasing werewolves," Jake said, pointing off into the woods.

Without another word, Jake's pet stalker took off to find Harley.

Chapter Twenty-seven

The staff meeting where everybody finally talked about her father's failure to get the state's approval for the creation of *Eureka!*—and his subsequent cover-up—had not been quite as bad as E.D. had expected. Jake's idea to have everybody think for a while first might have worked.

In spite of the shouting and recriminations and character assassination with which the discussion had begun, the family had come around surprisingly fast to a somewhat grudging willingness to face the crisis together. Lucille had decided that the orbs that were showing up in Harley's photographs were benevolent spirits who had come specifically to support their work, so she kept reminding everyone that there were cosmic forces on their side and there was absolutely nothing to worry about. She also shared Harley's idea about distraction and delay.

Once they'd quit criticizing Randolph for not setting things up properly with the state in the first place, no one in the family turned out to be any more willing than he was to accept North Carolina's right to interfere with or regulate what they were doing. They quickly settled on thwarting that interference any way they could. "We need to keep this whole thing quiet, though," Randolph said. "We don't want the campers' parents to get wind of it."

"But we have to tell the campers," E.D. had insisted. "Otherwise, it's still a cover-up. And cover-ups are always a bad idea. If we really believe in a creative community, we have to tell them what's up."

Lucille agreed. "We have an opportunity here to model a creative, collaborative approach to handling a crisis. We must share all this with the campers first thing tomorrow morning and then listen to what they come up with. I guarantee you they'll have ideas. After all, who's better at distraction and delay than kids? Creativity. Individuality. Cooperation. Isn't that the whole point of the camp?"

Even Randolph had agreed to this, on the condition that Lucille would do the talking and he didn't have to be there.

"I'll tell them about it after yoga, when everyone's fresh and energized," Lucille promised. "You'll see—their ideas will at least be worth listening to."

So E.D. had gone to yoga and struggled her way through it, hoping David wasn't watching as she kept tipping out of tree pose and had to bend her knees to touch the ground after waterfall. It wasn't until the final pose, when Jake, Destiny, and Winston came around the corner of the barn, that she realized she could have just shown up at the end to hear what Lucille would say and how the campers would take it. Winston flopped down in the shade of a sweet gum tree and lay with his head on his paws, watching. Jake and Destiny did the corpse posture (the only one E.D. did really well) with everyone else at the end, Destiny talking all the time about how fun it was to lie down and play dead when all the time you knew you were going to sit up afterward instead of getting "buried under the dirt with flowers on you."

When Lucille had rung the chimes to bring them back to sitting position, she announced that she had something to tell them and she wanted all of them, including Destiny, to just listen. They did.

"The state can make an unannounced inspection," Lucille said, wrapping up the story. "E.D. saw a man by the pond taking notes, but there's much more to a state inspection than that. So we're pretty sure he'll be back."

"If we fail the inspection, will they shut down the camp?" Q asked.

"Shut it down?" Destiny burst into tears. "No, no, no! I'm not finished the Petunia Possum drawings. And Cimmamon doesn't got all the words done, either."

"Archie and Hal just got the scaffolding up for my mural!" Samantha said, pointing to the side of the barn where a platform was rigged with ropes and pulleys. "I haven't even started it!"

"Harley's doing music for my lyrics!" Ginger said. "I want to have one of our songs in the end-of-camp show! If they shut us down, there won't *be* a show!"

"There *has* to be a show!" David said. "My mom's hiring a videographer to make a DVD. It's supposed to be my professional audition piece!"

"And Cordelia and I have been working on a way to combine Step with ballet," Q said. "We're going to revolutionize the world of dance!"

"Take it easy, everybody," Lucille said. "Breathe! We may be on the state's radar screen, but nothing has really happened yet. Tell them about distraction and delay, Harley."

When Harley had explained that they couldn't fail an inspection that hadn't been completed, E.D. told them that what they needed to do was think of ways to keep the inspector from getting it done. "He was probably just taking preliminary notes. An inspection includes collecting a water sample from the pond for testing, and I'm sure he hasn't done that yet. We need to keep it that way."

"So what do we do if he shows up at the pond to get some water?" Cinnamon asked. "Shoot him and sink his body in the muck?"

"Now there's an idea!" David said.

"That's what would happen in a Petunia Grantham mystery!" Cinnamon pointed out.

"This is *not* a Petunia Grantham mystery," Lucille said.

"Maybe we could keep him from getting to the pond in the first place," Q said. "How about we string trip wires across the trails and through the woods?"

"Oh sure, trip wires!" David said. "*That'll* stop an agent of the state."

E.D. sighed. She was beginning to wish her hormones would go back to wherever they came from. She suspected that Botticelli must have had nicer models for his angels.

"We could weave Elf Nets across the trails," Samantha said.

"*Elf* Nets?" David scoffed. "What the heck are Elf Nets?"

"Nets made out of vines and strung between trees.

Like the sculpture I made in Archie's workshop."

"She used honeysuckle and wisteria vines," E.D. said, "but if we wore gloves—and shirts with long sleeves—while we worked, we could use barbed wire vine and maybe even poison ivy, too. Nobody would dare try to get through a net like that. We could block every single trail in from the road. Maybe it wouldn't stop him completely, but it would sure slow him down."

"What if he comes through the meadow instead of the woods?" Ginger said.

"We could let Wolfie out of the goat pen," Destiny put in. "That would scare him away. Wolfie scares everybody."

"If he's sneaking around, how will we even know when he comes back?" Q asked. "He could show up anytime and anyplace. We need some kind of watch system."

"Winston! Winston!" Destiny said. "He always barks at strangers." Hearing his name, the dog looked up and thumped his tail. "See? Winston wants to be a watch system."

Jake nodded. "He could do it, but he'd have to see or hear or smell the guy. I guess he and I could take a walk around Wit's End a couple of times a day."

"Me, too! Me, too! I wants to go along!"

"We could all take turns," Q said. "We could walk the perimeter every hour or two. The dog could use the exercise."

"We could put 'walk the dog' on the Community Service list," David said. "That would be a heck of a lot better than cleaning bathrooms!"

Aside from vetoing murder, Aunt Lucille let the kids go on spinning out methods for distraction and delay without comment. She was listening in a way that E.D. recognized. The Applewhites believed in individual initiative and independence. She had a feeling the adults were going to let the kids do whatever they could think of short of murder and mayhem. She remembered a term from a program she had seen on television: *plausible deniability*. This way, if things went wrong somehow, the adults could all say they hadn't known about any of it. It was just a bunch of kids goofing around behind their backs. What the kids needed to do was make sure things didn't go wrong.

Chapter Twenty-eight

"Jake, Jake!" Harley's voice came over the walkie-talkie. "Code red! Winston's barking his head off."

This was it, Jake thought, his stomach starting to knot. It was July 11, four days since they'd started planning, and the man in the suit hadn't been spotted once. They'd developed Plans A through F to distract and delay the inspector no matter where or when he showed up, and the adults were letting them use the walkie-talkies to keep in touch. All the kids—including Hal and

Cordelia—had spent their mornings, wearing gardening gloves and sweating in long-sleeved shirts and jeans, building Elf Nets across the woods trails. They'd finished the last one just this morning. The rest of the time, except for the perimeter dog walks, camp had gone on as usual, E.D. coming up with daily schedules that managed to fit the workshops into the afternoons, with theater, as usual, taking up the evenings. Nobody expected an inspector to come after dinner.

Jake had been hoping the inspector wouldn't come back. The truth was, he'd had enough run-ins with state government to last the rest of his life. Rhode Island had banned him from public school and put him in foster care. He wasn't looking forward to trouble with North Carolina. At least this time, he reminded himself, it wasn't Jake Semple alone against a whole state. He figured he was pretty much an innocent bystander.

"Did you hear me, Jake? Code red!"

"Roger," Jake said. "Where are you?"

"Meadow. Not far from the goat pen."

"Ten-four. Meadow's Plan C. Can you see him?"

"Guy in a suit. Heading in from the road."

"Has he seen you?"

"Don't know. He can't miss the barking!"

"Okay. Stay out of sight if you can. But don't lose him. I'll get the others on it."

Jake wished there were enough walkie-talkies for everybody to have one, but Randolph had vetoed buying more. In the afternoons the campers tended to be scattered all over camp. He'd been printing out song lyrics in the office when Harley called in. Now he looked at the Wit's End map on the wall and checked the afternoon schedule. This was the first after-lunch session of the day, which meant Ginger was in Wisteria Cottage with Lucille.

Samantha was at work on the scaffolding at the barn. Harley had finished his photomontage. Samantha had laid out the patchwork pattern on the barn wall and should be painting her mural now. Cordelia, Q, and David were in the dance studio, probably arguing, as usual, over the best way to create a fusion of Step, tap, and ballet. And Cinnamon—*perfect!*—Cinnamon was at the goat pen already, where she was supposedly trying to tame Wolfie so the Petunia Possum picture book could have a happy ending. The inspector's route and timing couldn't be better for Plan C. He thumbed the walkie-talkie to transmit. "Cinnamon! Did you hear? He's somewhere near you."

There was a brief crackle of static. Then "Roger that. I've spotted the target. Ten-four. Waiting for him to get closer."

The only person Jake couldn't locate on the schedule was E.D. But she had a walkie-talkie with her. He hoped she had it turned on. "E.D. Where are you?"

"Dance studio."

The dance studio. David was there. Was she still hung up on that jerk? "Mobilizing Plan C. Blue already in place. Step One about to begin."

"I heard. Cordelia, David, and Q on their way. I'm heading for Wisteria to change Green Twin to Blue and deploy. Cinnamon!"

"Yep?"

"Got your scarf with you?"

"Yep."

Destiny was going to be terribly disappointed to have missed this, Jake thought. He'd wanted to be part of what he called "destruction and delay." He'd been carrying an empty single-portion cereal box around with him, calling it his "walkie-talker." But Sybil had taken him with her to the library in town to get more kids' books for her market research. "I'm a nil-ustrator," he'd told Jake importantly as he climbed into the car after lunch with a backpack to fill with picture books. "I gots to do research too."

Jake hurried out of the office and ran toward the goat pen. Step One for Plan C was the release of Wolfie, and he didn't want to miss it. After that, of course, though everybody had a job to do, they had to be flexible and creative. Once Wolfie was loose, there was no way to predict how things would unfold.

As he got closer, he could hear barking and

shouting. He arrived at the goat pen out of breath and sweating. Cinnamon was standing by the open gate. Hazel was next to her, nibbling contemplatively at the hem of Cinnamon's shorts. All the action was in the meadow. Harley was shouting at Winston, who was chasing Wolfie, who was chasing a man in a dark suit, who was dodging around among the waist-high weeds and grass and thistles, flapping a clipboard behind him and hollering for someone to "Call him off, call him off!"

"Run for the woods!" Harley shouted at the man now. "It's your only hope!"

Dodging and weaving, the man began angling toward the trees on the other side of the meadow, Wolfie closing on him fast. The man caught sight of the beginning of a trail and headed for it, putting on a final burst of speed, apparently thinking, from Harley's warning, that Wolfie would stop once he got in under the trees. Wolfie, of course, would not stop. But the man would, Jake knew. Not more than ten yards into the woods an Elf Net was strung securely across the trail.

Sure enough, there was a scream just about the time Wolfie headed in among the trees and then another—louder and more bloodcurdling—as Wolfie apparently caught up to the inspector, who was surely caught in, or at least stopped by, the Elf Net. It occurred to Jake that injuring a representative of the government was probably not a good idea. But he need not have worried. Cinnamon put two fingers in her mouth and whistled a whistle that could have been heard in the next county. A moment later Wolfie appeared at the edge of the meadow, a narrow strip of dark fabric caught on his twisted horn.

"Stay where you are, mister!" Harley shouted toward the woods, "while we catch the goat. Don't come out till we say it's okay!" It wasn't an instruction the man was likely to ignore. Cinnamon, with Hazel at her heels, hurried across the meadow to meet Wolfie.

Jake could hardly believe his eyes as he watched Wolfie fall in next to Hazel and the two goats trot docilely after Cinnamon straight back into the pen. Too bad Lucille wasn't here to see, he thought. Cinnamon, the goat-whisperer, slipped into the shed and returned with a coffee can full of feed, which she poured on the ground. As the goats began to eat, she went out of the pen and closed the gate. By that time Ginger had arrived, dressed now in blue, a matching scarf securely covering her Mohawk haircut. Cinnamon whipped an identical scarf out of her pocket and tied it on over her red curls. The two girls now looked exactly alike. Destiny could probably tell them apart, Jake thought, but nobody else could.

He pushed the transmitter button on his walkie-talkie. "Samantha. Blue and Blue deployed."

"Roger. I'll be ready if he comes this way."

What happened next would depend on the twins. Cinnamon would go down the trail and ask the inspector where he wanted to go. Then she'd offer to take him on a shortcut through the woods. After that she and Ginger would take turns disappearing and popping up in unexpected places. When he'd seen Cinnamon disappear behind a tangle of bushes and vines in one direction, Ginger was to pop up in the opposite direction and ask why he was going that way. By the time he got out of the woods, they figured he'd be doubting his sanity. Depending on the route they were able to pick out, which was something they hadn't been able to plan, they might lead him to the barn, where Samantha could accidentally spill a can of paint down on him from the scaffolding, or back to the meadow, where Q and David would be ready to open the gate and turn Wolfie loose again.

When they'd planned it originally, they weren't sure how David and Q would get Wolfie back once he was free, but now it was clear they'd only need Cinnamon to come and whistle for him. *How did she do that?* Jake wondered.

There wasn't anything more for Jake to do now except wait either to see the man emerge into the meadow again or to hear from Samantha that she'd dumped paint on his head. Distraction and delay. So far, so good. If he were the guy stuck in the Elf Net, Jake thought, he wouldn't be any too eager to come back to Wit's End—ever.

Chapter Twenty-nine

E.D. missed the whole of Plan C. When she'd arrived at Wisteria Cottage, Ginger and Lucille had been poring over a book of folk songs, comparing verses and choruses and talking about the uses of repetition in songwriting. "Code red!" she shouted as she went in. "The inspector's back—in the meadow! Plan C has started already. You need to change clothes, Ginger, and get out there as fast as you can."

"It's okay, go!" Lucille said. Ginger turned and ran for Dogwood Cottage. "Plan C?"

"Plausible deniability," E.D. said. "You don't want to know."

"Nobody will get hurt, right?"

"That'll pretty much depend on Wolfie," E.D. said as she headed for the door. She wanted to get back in time to see the action.

"Wait!" Lucille said. "I want you to look at something."

"But I have to go—"

"Do you play a central role in Plan C?"

"No—but—"

"Okay, then. This'll only take a minute." Lucille pulled E.D. over to Archie's laptop on the kitchen table. She didn't let go of her arm as she brought a photograph up on the screen. "I'm thinking of starting a blog about all this. Something wonderful is happening. I've already written three poems. It's not just Harley's camera. Look here!"

That was how E.D. missed what happened in the meadow. Lucille insisted on showing her all the evidence that orbs couldn't be accounted for by the camera flash lighting up dust particles or moisture in the air. Lucille and Harley had been conducting experiments. They'd stirred up dust in the storage rooms of the barn and taken pictures. Those photos had some orblike blobs, but they all were fuzzy and indistinct. None of them had the interior mandala patterns, and none of them had blue fringes. They'd run the shower in Wisteria's bathroom until the room was full of mist, and none of the photos they'd taken had orbs in them at all. There were even two photos with colored orbs that had been taken outside without a flash. *Incontrovertible evidence,* Lucille called these photographs.

"But the best thing of all," she announced with triumph, "is that you can *call* them! At least I can. Harley refused to try."

"Well, thanks for showing me these," E.D. said. "But I really should get back—"

"Just a few more! Look here."

E.D. sighed. "I don't see any orbs."

Lucille nodded. "Exactly! There weren't any. So I closed my eyes, went into a meditative state, and asked them to show up and let us take their picture. And they came! I'm afraid Harley's a little freaked by it all. He's considering giving up photography altogether."

By the time E.D. finally managed to get away, she found Jake and the campers at the goat pen, congratulating themselves on their success and complaining about the things that hadn't worked the way they'd expected.

It turned out that Ginger and Cinnamon had gotten themselves just as lost in the woods as the inspector until Ginger finally stumbled onto the road by accident. As soon as the man had seen pavement, he took off running, or at least limping very fast, to find his car. "I think Wolfie must have hurt the man's leg a little when he tore his pants," Ginger said.

"So we didn't get to sic Wolfie on him again," David said. "Too bad! I don't think he even drew blood the first time."

"And Samantha didn't get to dump her paint," Jake added.

"I'm just as glad," Samantha said. "I'd finally managed to get the colors right, and I didn't want to waste the paint. Besides, I got four whole patches of the barn quilt finished. You all need to come see it!"

"Archie's gone to the pond. He's giving us an extra optional swim," Q said. "Cordelia went to get Hal and change into her suit." The others agreed they were more than ready for a swim.

E.D. had still not convinced herself that the pond was okay for swimming, so while the others went to change into their suits, she headed back to the air-conditioned office. She'd been thinking about Aunt Lucille and Harley looking for evidence about orbs, and realized there was still no evidence that the messages that had continued to appear in the mailbox were real. She'd never actually gotten around to checking. If the whole thing was really Mrs. Montrose trying to get revenge on her father, it could be that the woman had exaggerated the danger. Maybe the state couldn't actually shut them down at all. The thing to do was go online and check out the North Carolina Department of Environment and Natural Resources.

Before they harassed a state inspector again, it would be a good idea to know for sure how much was riding on his report.

Fifteen minutes later, E.D. had found the regulations. They had not been exaggerated. Not only were they word for word what the messages had said, there were pages and pages more. On the department's home page she had also found the phone number for customer relations, and that gave her an idea. If she pretended to be someone reporting violations, she might be able to find out exactly what the state could and would do about them. And maybe, even more important, how much time it would take them to do it.

E.D. picked up the phone and put it down again. Calling a government office was scary. Then she remembered the improv exercise. As bad as she was at acting, she was really pretty good at improvising. *I can do this!* she thought. She would pretend to be somebody like Mrs. Montrose. She would call in to report violations at some anonymous camp and just see what happened. She took a deep breath, picked up the phone, and dialed the customer service number.

When a friendly voice answered, E.D. lowered her voice, doing her best to sound like her mother. "I'd like to talk to whoever is in charge of regulating camps in North Carolina," she said.

"Resident camps?" the friendly voice asked.

"Yes—resident camps."

"That would be Joseph Gant. He is out of the office at the moment, but I can connect you with his assistant, Daryl Gaffney. One moment. I'll put you through."

It was working, E.D. thought. The woman hadn't acted as if she was talking to a kid. "This is Daryl Gaffney, how may I help you?"

"Mr. Gaffney," E.D. said in her best Sybil voice, "I have some questions about possible rule violations at a summer camp."

"What sorts of violations?"

"There are several. Vermin infestation, for instance." She thought about Paulie in the kitchen while Aunt Lucille and her mother fixed meals. That was absolutely against the sanitary regulations. "Live animals in the kitchen during meal preparation. Unsanitary conditions in living quarters. I think your department should send an inspector to investigate this facility immediately."

There was a slight pause before Mr. Gaffney responded. "I missed your name, Ms. . . . ."

"My name is . . . Sybil . . ." E.D. looked wildly around the office for a possible last name. A dictionary was leaning against the printer. "Sybil Webster."

"Well, Ms. Webster, our department does not actually conduct those inspections. They are done by the county health department in the county where the camp is located. Such inspections are, of course, done *for* the state, which issues the camp permits, but not *by* the state. How large a camp is this?"

"Sixteen acres," E.D. said.

There was a muffled chuckle on the other end of the line. "I'm sorry, ma'am—I meant how many campers are served by the facility?"

"Six."

"Six? You mean six *hundred*? On sixteen acres?"

"No. I mean six. Six campers."

Now there was no question that Mr. Gaffney was doing his best to suppress a laugh. He wasn't quite succeeding. "I'm very sorry, Ms. Webster, but as you may know, the state of North Carolina, like most states, works under considerable budgetary restraint. We are snowed under with regulations—there's the ban on smoking in public restaurants and bars, for instance—a nightmare, that one! There simply isn't the staff to enforce them all. We do our best, but you really have no idea how many regulations we and the county health departments have to deal with! We are stretched very, very thin! *Six campers!* Has anyone become ill at this camp? Has anyone—*died*?"

"Certainly not!"

"Then, Ms. Webster, I suggest you begin by taking up the issue with the camp management. Ask them to clean up their act, as it were. Ask them to call in exterminators. And get the animals out of the kitchen. If you could see the load of casework we deal with at our end, you'd understand that a situation of this—this— Is there such a word as *minitude?* The opposite, I mean to say, of *magnitude?* Well, I mean, I just have to tell you that a camp of that size is not going to readily make its way to the top of our workload. Or that of the particular county's health department, for that matter." Daryl Gaffney was openly chuckling now. "Is there—is there anything else I can help you with?"

"No, thank you," E.D. said. "I appreciate you taking the time to speak to me."

"Think nothing of it," Mr. Gaffney said. "You've been a breath of fresh air in a very dull day. *Six campers!"*

He was laughing outright when E.D. hung up. The regulations were real. But if the state—or the county health department—didn't have the staff to enforce them, *who was the man in the suit?*

Chapter Thirty

Destiny hadn't gotten back from the library in time to swim, so Jake had been free to swim with the campers. He'd taken Winston along, and the dog was so exhausted that once he'd gotten a drink from the pond edge, he dragged his muddy body back, flopped down in the shade, and went instantly to sleep.

Not once during the whole of optional swim did Jake catch Ginger staring at him with that look of adoration. As relieved as he was, Jake had to admit to himself that he was almost sorry. Nobody in his life had ever looked at him that way before. He pretty much doubted it would ever happen again.

With Archie overseeing the water activities, they staged individual races, most of which Q won; relay races with endless arguments over who should be on which team and whether the fastest swimmers on a team should go first or last; a diving contest, which David won with a forward front flip that Jake could hardly believe could be done without a diving board; and finally a game of Marco Polo that went badly wrong when Samantha, Cinnamon, and Ginger accused David of cheating. The argument over that got so heated that Archie kicked everybody out of the pond fifteen minutes early.

The twins said everybody should go see Samantha's mural; David stormed off to the boys' cottage by himself; and the others, except for Hal, who reluctantly went to keep an eye on David, gathered their sandals and towels and set off toward the barn.

As Jake started after them, Harley hung back. "Can I talk to you?" he said. "Privately?"

"Sure! What's up?"

"Well. Um." Harley fiddled with the towel around his neck. "You know how I told you I don't sing?"

"Yeah."

"See, the thing is—I sort of do. I mean, I really do—I *can*—but I don't. I mean I haven't." He rubbed his nose. "I've spent my whole life on the road with my folks, going from concert to concert. I was 'bus schooled,' is how my mom puts it. There were never any other kids in my life—just my parents and the band and their fans. I didn't get much chance to be a kid."

Jake nodded. As different as his life had been from Harley's, he sort of knew how that was.

"So I decided when I was still pretty little that the way to be *me* was to not be *them*. I learned to play the guitar way back before I figured out the 'me' thing, but I don't carry one around with me or anything. Since I didn't want to sing, I was gonna be a painter till I found out I wasn't any good at it, and then I decided to do photography instead."

"But you *can* sing?"

"Oh, yeah. I can. So what I wanted to ask is, Is it too late to join your workshop?"

Jake laughed. "As long as you don't expect much from me as a singing coach. We just all sort of figure stuff out together."

"It's not so much for the singing part. You know the music that came into my head for Ginger's lyrics? Well, I was thinking she and I might be able to sing a duet at the end-of-camp show. I mean, if we have an end-of-camp show. If the state doesn't shut us down or anything. Trouble is, I didn't bring my guitar—"

"Archie has one," Jake said.

"I didn't know he plays the guitar."

"He doesn't. He bought it a long time ago when he was going around the world on a tramp steamer. Thought he'd learn to play and use it to impress girls." Jake chuckled. "He learned a few chords; but since he doesn't sing, the whole thing just never worked out. He's still got it though. It's in a closet in Wisteria Cottage. I'm pretty sure he'd lend it to you."

Archie had just swum across the pond from the diving platform and was climbing onto the dock. "Go ask him," Jake said. "We could definitely use somebody in the workshop who can play live music for us! Are you any good?"

Harley nodded. "The bass guitarist told me I was a prodigy."

"Be careful of that word," Jake said. "Go ask!"

After they'd all checked out Samantha's mural, which was really big, really original, a little strange, and— everybody agreed—really good, Jake, with Winston tagging behind, went back to Wisteria Cottage to shower and change. When he got there, Archie had dug out his guitar and dusted off the case.

"It's about time this old thing got some use!" he said. "So Harley's a guitar prodigy, huh? Lucille's right. This group just gets more and more interesting. Have you seen Samantha's mural?"

Jake nodded. "It seems pretty good to me. I don't

know that much about art—"

"One thing's for sure: when it's done, we're going to have ourselves the most unusual barn in the state! If the government doesn't close us down, I'm thinking we could sell tickets to the end-of-camp show. Would you take this to Harley?"

E.D. was heading up the steps of Wisteria Cottage when Jake and Winston came out later. "We have to talk," E.D. said, waving at the rocking chairs on the porch. "Sit!" Winston sat. So did Jake. From the look on E.D.'s face, there was just no point in arguing.

"So, if this guy isn't a state inspector," Jake said when she finished telling him about her call to the department, "who *is* he?"

"That's what *I* want to know!"

"We should tell your folks. No sense letting them go on worrying that the state could come swooping down on us any minute."

E.D. didn't answer at first. She just stared off into the trees for a while. Then she smiled in a way that looked to Jake more conspiratorial than cheery. "I'm thinking it wouldn't hurt to let them go on worrying awhile. After all, they're the grown-ups here—the talented, creative, famous grown-ups! And not one of them thought to check with the state before they put everybody to the trouble of creating the camp! And bringing in the campers! Now that *I* know we aren't in danger, I don't mind at all that they still think we are. Serves Dad right when you come right down to it. All I want is to find out who this guy really is."

"After what happened to him today, you expect him to come back?"

E.D. shrugged. "Let's see if the messages keep turning up in the mailbox. If so, it means the charade continues. So we go on keeping watch. Then—if he comes back—instead of chasing him off, we need to catch him and get the whole story."

Jake looked at Winston, who was asleep again, snoring noisily. "Winston's practically worn to the bone tromping around the whole of Wit's End four times a day. He's so exhausted that a butterfly actually landed on his head this afternoon and he didn't do a thing."

"It's about time he figured out he's never going to catch one. Winston's not worn to the bone; he's just lost a little weight. That dog's in better shape than he's been since he was a puppy."

Jake thought about what had changed since E.D. had found the threatening messages and caught sight of the guy in the suit. When they'd thought there was a threat to the camp, everybody had started pulling together. Even David and Q had begun cooperating, at least occasionally. The threat really had turned them—adults and kids alike—into an ensemble, all focused on the same thing. "Okay.

So what do we do instead of distraction and delay?"

"I don't know yet."

"Harley's joining my singing workshop, so if you bring Hal and Cordelia to the next one, we can tell everybody together."

Chapter Thirty-one

For almost a week the messages went on showing up with the mail, and E.D. took guilty delight in watching her father prowl around Wit's End obsessing over mess and looking for signs of vermin infestation. He was the only one who still seemed to be taking the threat seriously. When the results of Plan C had been reported at a staff meeting, Zedediah said they might as well just go on taking things a day at a time. "We haven't heard directly from the state, after all. I doubt that we'll see the man again. It's hard to imagine that a little operation like ours will seem worth risking life and limb over."

Lucille insisted there was no need to worry in any case since they were so clearly under the protection of cosmic forces. She had taken to keeping her camera with her all the time and taking sudden flash photographs without warning. "We are positively surrounded by orbs!"

Then, very early on the morning of July 17, when all the campers were at yoga, Sybil was in the kitchen getting breakfast, and E.D. was putting up the daily schedule in the dining tent, the plain black car came up the drive and pulled to a stop by the front porch with a squeal of brakes. The man, this time wearing a light blue suit, emerged from the car with his clipboard in hand and leaned on the horn.

E.D. flipped on her walkie-talkie. She hoped Jake was awake and that wherever he was, he had his walkie-talkie with him. "Jake! Jake, are you on? 9-1-1. Repeat. 9-1-1. Come to the Lodge. Right now!"

At the sound of the horn, Paulie, in the kitchen, had begun screaming like someone being attacked by an ax murderer. The horn, beeping over and over, had apparently sent him into a frenzy. Sybil hurried to the door and came out on the porch, wiping her hands on her apron. "May I help you?"

"I'm from the Department of Environment and Natural Resources!" the man shouted over the sound of Paulie's screams. "Who's in charge here?"

"Well I suppose I am at the moment," Sybil said. "I'm the associate director."

He waggled an official-looking name tag at her. "I'm Thomas Timmons, and I've come to inspect this camp." He looked at his clipboard. *"Eureka!* Is that the name? Strange name for a camp."

"Inspect the camp?" Sybil said as if she'd never heard of such a thing. "We've had no call about an inspection!"

"Of course you haven't had a call. This is an unannounced inspection, as per Section 15A of the North Carolina Administrative Code. What is there about the term 'unannounced' you don't understand?"

Paulie's screams subsided, and he began instead a series of his most colorful curses.

"Am I correct in assuming that someone at this camp is swearing at an agent of the government? I will not be sworn at!" Brandishing his clipboard, the man stormed up the steps of the porch, and Sybil retreated until she was backed up against the screen door.

"That's just Paulie," she said. "My father-in-law's parrot."

"Parrot?" The man pulled a pen from his jacket pocket and jotted something on the clipboard. "A live bird on the premises. Clear danger of psittacosis. I hope this bird does not reside in the kitchen. That would be a serious violation of regulations!"

Sybil's face drained of color. "Reside? Well, no! Paulie *resides* in Maple Cottage. He was just brought over this morning to be—"

"This is to be a full inspection: food preparation area, lodging facilities, sanitation and bathing facilities, drinking water, vermin control, recreational waters. All of it. The future of this camp will depend on the results. I wish to begin with food preparation. Take me to your kitchen!"

"What is that infernal racket?" Randolph's voice could be heard now amid Paulie's gradually diminishing shrieks and curses. "Doesn't anyone down there know what time it is? It is barely past dawn!"

At that moment Winston came around the house barking his terrorist protection bark. Jake hurried after him, walkie-talkie in hand. Destiny, still in his pajamas, followed.

"Someone put up that dog!" the man yelled over the tumult. "It is against the law for an unrestrained animal to be present during an official inspection."

"Jake!" Sybil said. "Take Winston somewhere else, would you please?"

"Is that the *bad man*, Mommy?" Destiny demanded. "The *destruction and delay* man?"

"Hush, Destiny. Of course not," Sybil said.

"Come on, Winston!" E.D. called. "You too, Destiny."

If they were to put the plan they had come up with into effect, she had to let the others know what was going on. "Let's go watch the campers do yoga!"

"Oooh, goodie! Can I do it, too? I'm really, really good at yoga," Destiny told the man as E.D. grabbed his hand and tried to aim him toward the barn, "but they never lets me do it. They say I'm too loud. Am I too loud, do you think?"

By this time Randolph, in undershorts and T-shirt, had come to the door, smoothing his tangled hair. "What's all this? Who are you?"

"Thomas Timmons, from the Department of Environment and Natural Resources!" the man repeated, glancing over his shoulder from time to time at Winston, who was now growling menacingly and uttering the occasional *woof* as he followed E.D.

"Then I suggest you go look after the environment. Get out there and protect some of our natural resources and quit intruding on the affairs of the citizens of this state whose taxes are responsible for keeping you employed."

The man waved his clipboard again. "I *demand* to be taken to your kitchen. Immediately!"

Jake hurried to the porch steps. "Excuse me, sir," he said. "But the campers haven't had breakfast yet, so the kitchen is very busy at the moment. I'd be happy to take you to see the lodging facilities, and we can come back to the kitchen when the campers are eating. The food preparation area won't go anywhere while we're gone, I promise you."

"I want you to know that I'm calling your superiors!" Randolph blustered through the screen door now. "It's a crime to send anyone here before normal work hours. *Eureka!* is not open to the public until ten o'clock, I'll have you know!"

"Randolph! Go upstairs and get dressed," Sybil was saying as E.D. pulled Destiny away.

Chapter Thirty-two

wo can play at this game, Jake thought as he led the still-blustering Thomas Timmons, or whatever his name really was, on as roundabout a route as he could manage past the far side of the Lodge toward the boys' and girls' cottages. He began explaining *Eureka!* as if he really believed the man was an inspector from the state.

"This used to be a motor lodge," he told him, "so the campers stay in self-contained cottages. Each one houses three campers and a counselor and has a full kitchen and a full bath. Even though the cottages aren't air-conditioned, we like to think *Eureka!*

provides exceptionally luxurious accommodations."

"The department doesn't care about luxury," the man said, scratching the back of his neck with one hand. His frown got even more ferocious. "What we care about is the health and well-being of the campers. What we care about is sanitation. Sanitation and *safety*!"

Jake hoped this guy's intimidating attitude was all an act. If the plan they'd figured out—the plan he hoped E.D. was getting organized right now—was going to work, the man pretty much had to be a good guy at heart.

When they'd gathered to figure out what to do, David had suggested replacing distraction and delay with "capture and torture."

Q had accused him of watching too much television, but Cinnamon pointed out that the capture part was right. "We need to catch him instead of chasing him off. But how?"

Destiny had started jumping up and down. "I know how, I know how! We can dig a Heffalump trap. Like Pooh and Piglet. We can dig a *pit* where he'll fall in and he won't be able to get out."

Everyone had laughed at this at first. But it was Destiny's Heffalump trap that finally led them to their plan. Of course, they had thought the man would sneak into Wit's End the way he had before. They hadn't expected him to make a frontal assault. But now that he had, they would just have to make the best of it. *Creativity and flexibility,* Jake thought. *Like Zedediah said.* Jake figured his job was to stall for time and give the man a false sense of confidence. Thomas Timmons needed to believe they were buying his act.

The two of them had arrived at the boys' cottage now, and Jake led the man onto the porch. "You'll be interested in the Community Service aspect of the *Eureka!* program. We've involved every person at the camp, staff and campers alike, in making sure that everything is kept clean and in order." With that he opened the door so that the man could go inside. *It's a good thing this isn't real!* Jake thought. Nothing about what greeted them as they entered was clean and in order.

Because Hal needed a room of his own, Harley had been sleeping on a foldout couch in the living room. Not only was the couch-bed not made, but the tangle of bedclothes was strewn with pages of music, some of it printed, some handwritten, and Archie's guitar lay on top of it all. The guitar case was open on the kitchen table, and empty soda bottles and glasses littered the counter. The mess was clearly not Harley's alone. There were clothes, dirty socks, smelly sneakers, and wet towels strewn on the floor, along with a pair of men's ballet slippers and one tap shoe. A flowerpot filled with sand supported a dead branch festooned with tangles of equally dead honeysuckle where someone had been practicing weaving Elf Nets.

Thomas Timmons whipped out his pen and began making marks on the sheets of paper clipped to his board, clicking his tongue and shaking his head. Jake bit his lip to keep from laughing and led the way down the hall to Hal's room, and David and Q's, both of which made the living room look neat by comparison. He had decided to save the bathroom for last.

Chapter Thirty-three

When E.D., Winston, and Destiny approached the parking area in the shadow of the barn, the barefoot campers and Cordelia were in a semicircle around Lucille doing tree pose. Lucille, Cordelia, and Samantha were each standing perfectly balanced on one leg, the other foot flat against the inside of the knee and their hands entwined above their heads, gazing raptly skyward. Nobody else had managed to look up. Most of them were teetering on one leg and waving their arms and hands in the air to try to maintain balance.

"Aunt Lucille, Aunt Lucille!" E.D. shouted. It was as if the sound knocked them all over. Even Lucille tipped sideways and stepped out of the pose. "There's a state inspector demanding to see the kitchen!"

"What? An inspector? Now? Good heavens, not the kitchen!"

"Jake took him off to the bunks first, but Mom needs help!"

"Cordelia!" Lucille said, pushing her feet into her flip-flops and snatching up her water bottle. "Can you finish the yoga session? Just do one sun salutation, I think." She was off even before Cordelia could answer, running toward the Lodge.

"This is it," E.D. told the others when she was sure her aunt was out of earshot. "He drove right up to the Lodge and identified himself as the state inspector. Has a fake ID and everything. Mom's freaking, Dad's furious. They have no idea, of course, that he isn't what he says he is. Jake's stalling him—letting him do his inspector act at the bunks. We have time to get ready, but we have to hurry. Have you got your camera, Harley?"

Harley grabbed it and held it up.

"Good. Destiny? Do you remember what you're supposed to do?"

"I'm the honeypot!" Destiny said. "For the bottom of the pit. 'Cept I gotta yell and yell."

"Where's your life jacket?"

"We left it by the dock," Ginger said, "so it would be there when we needed it."

"I'll go get Wolfie," Cinnamon said.

"Be sure to keep him out of sight—and leave him on his rope till we see if we need him. Destiny could be enough."

"Yeah, yeah, I know. We don't want to chase the guy away again."

E.D. checked her watch. "I don't know how long it'll take for him to inspect the cottages. . . ."

"If Dogwood's as bad as ours, it'll take a while," Q said.

"It's pretty bad," Cordelia said. "I'll run over and lead him through it—pretend I'm afraid of what he's going to report. This is going to be fun."

"There are still mouse turds in our room," Ginger said. "Act as if you're trying to hide them so he'll be sure to notice."

As Cordelia started away, E.D. called to her. "Tell Jake to beep my walkie-talkie when you're done at the cottages. You can say you'll take the guy to the pond before he goes back to inspect the kitchen. I'll meet you all on your way there."

"Ten-four!"

"Everybody remember what you're supposed to do?" E.D. asked.

"Gee, no, we're all idiots," David said.

That, E.D. thought, was enough. Hormones or no

hormones, she was finished with David! What had she *ever* seen in him? "Let's go!"

"I gots to get my swimming suit!" Destiny said.

"No time for that. You can go in your pajamas," E.D. told him.

"Head 'em up, move 'em out," Q shouted.

"All for one and one for all," Harley called as they started toward the pond.

Chapter Thirty-four

Once Cordelia arrived it got harder and harder for Jake to keep a straight face. She came tearing up the path and stood in front of the door of Dogwood Cottage with her arms folded across her chest. "You can't come in here," she told the man. "We're not ready."

"That is the point of an unannounced inspection," the man said. His voice, Jake thought, had softened suddenly. Cordelia, in her yoga outfit, her hair curling damply around her face, was looking particularly gorgeous. "We need to see conditions as they really are, not as they've been fixed up to impress us."

Cordelia, with a great show of reluctance, moved aside and let him open the door.

Jake hadn't been inside the girls' cottage since the first night of camp. Except that here it was Cordelia who slept on the foldout couch, the scene inside was much more like the boys' cottage than he would have guessed. If anything, it was worse, mostly because the girls seemed to have a lot more clothes. Blue and green shirts and shorts, sneakers and sandals, jeans and T-shirts and bathing suits were draped on furniture and lay in piles on the floor, along with a surprising number of Cordelia's skirts and blouses. In the midst of the clothes were Samantha's books—piled, strewn, and stacked everywhere.

"Normally, it's much neater than this," Cordelia said, blushing slightly as she slipped some underwear under a blouse.

Thomas Timmons nodded. He seemed to be paying as much attention to Cordelia as to the mess he was inspecting. Alternating between jotting notes on the pages of his clipboard and using his pen to scratch his neck, he muttered "dreadful," "appalling," and "disgusting" under his breath. As he started down the hall, Cordelia whispered to Jake E.D.'s message about letting her know when they were finished here.

In the twins' room, Cordelia kept putting herself between Thomas Timmons and what he was trying to inspect as if she wanted to keep him from seeing something. Finally, he actually put out a hand and moved her, surprisingly gently, out of the way.

"Vermin!" he said triumphantly, pointing at the scattering of mouse droppings all along the baseboards and the small pile in the corner. "This cabin is infested with mice!"

"We're planning to get a cat!" Cordelia said, and Jake had to clamp a hand over his mouth and leave the room entirely.

When the man had taken more notes in the bathroom, which wasn't so much dirty, Jake thought, as incredibly cluttered with tubes and bottles and jars and various zippered bags, combs, and brushes covering every square inch of horizontal surface, they went out onto the porch and Jake pressed the key on his walkie-talkie that would let E.D. know they were coming. Cordelia asked what else the man needed to inspect.

"Everything, of course!" he said. "Except, perhaps the woods. I don't need to go hiking all over the whole sixteen acres."

"Shall we take you to see the goat pen?" she asked innocently.

"I think not," he said quickly. He made a show of flipping through the forms on his clipboard. "There is nothing in here about goat facilities."

"Okay, then," Cordelia said, starting down the path toward the pond. "We might as well take you to the pond. It's where we swim. Quite nice. Lovely clear water."

"I'll be the judge of that," the man said,. following closely behind her.

"After that we'll take you back to the Lodge so you can inspect the kitchen," Jake said, trailing along after them. "The campers should be gathering in the dining tent very soon for breakfast. This is a creativity camp. Tell him about our workshops, Cordelia. And the end-of-camp show we're planning."

"End-of-camp show? I hope you haven't spent a lot of energy on that!" the man said. "It's highly likely, given what I've seen so far, that the department will decide to close this camp down."

Cordelia yelped. "Close it down? Why? When? How?"

As the man talked, citing violation after violation, Cordelia led him on toward the pond until E.D. came hurtling up the path and crashed into them. She was out of breath, her face red and terrified.

"Oh, thank God. Come quick!" she yelled. "Destiny's fallen into the pond, and something's got him! I think it's a snapping turtle! The biggest one I've ever seen." She looked up at Thomas Timmons, clearly distraught. "Oh, please, please come and help us save my little brother! Snapping turtles can bite through a grown man's leg. What'll it do to a five-year-old? I tried to reach him, but I couldn't! Maybe you can! But hurry! Oh, please! Hurry, hurry, hurry!"

She turned around and tore off down the path. The man ran after her, and Jake and Cordelia closed in behind. No doubt about it, Jake thought, E.D. was really good at improvisation! He almost believed her himself.

As they got closer to the pond, they could hear Destiny shrieking at the top of his lungs. "Oww! Owwwww! It gots my foot. It hurts! Help, help, help! Somebody help! Oooowwww!"

Winston was standing belly-deep in the pond, barking.

Ginger and Samantha were running back and forth along the edge of the pond screaming about the monster that had hold of Destiny. "It's huge!"

"Even with his life jacket, it could pull him under!"

"He'll drown!"

"Or maybe bleed to death!"

"Oh, help, help, help!"

Out just a little way beyond the end of the dock, Destiny was splashing frantically and continuing to yell.

E.D. ran out to the end of the dock, crouched down, and reached toward Destiny. "You need to get closer," she shouted to him.

"I can't! Oooowwww! He gots me. I can't!"

Thomas Timmons threw down his clipboard, ran onto the dock, and moved E.D. out of his way. Then he knelt and stretched one arm toward Destiny, who went on screaming and splashing, still well out of reach. E.D. scuttled back off the dock as David and Q came running from the woods with the dock ropes they'd untied from the trees. Jake snatched away the ramp that led onto the dock while Cordelia, E.D., and the other two girls began shoving it out into the water. Harley came from the woods with his camera and started clicking one picture after another.

At the front of the dock Thomas Timmons, still focused entirely on the screaming and splashing in front of him, had taken off his suit jacket and was waving it at Destiny. "Here, here! Try to grab on to my jacket. If you can get it, I can pull you over."

As the dock floated steadily toward him, Destiny, still yelling and splashing, managed to paddle steadily backward. The others had stopped pushing now, but Jake and Cordelia, up to their knees in muck, gave one last tremendous shove. Thomas Timmons, having finally reached Destiny's hand, dropped his suit jacket on the dock behind him and pulled Destiny around to the ladder as the dock floated completely away from the shore.

Destiny stopped yelling and climbed the ladder

as the man got to his feet. "Thanks, oh thanks! The monster thingie letted me go!" he said. Then he pointed back toward the edge of the pond. "But we can't get back to the land anymore."

It wasn't until then that Thomas Timmons discovered he'd been caught in a Heffalump trap.

Chapter Thirty-five

Getting the man out of the Heffalump trap turned out to be considerably more difficult than getting him into it. As the dock floated away, it had dragged the ropes into the water, where they'd sunk immediately muck-ward, so there was no way to pull it back in. Destiny, not the least bit bothered by muck, jumped off the dock and paddled his way back till he could stand up and slog his way to solid ground, where a dripping Winston met him, wagging with relief, and shook pond water all over him.

"My idea worked! Did you see how good it worked?" Destiny burbled to E.D. as he unbuckled his muddy life jacket. "I was a very good honeypot. Don't you think I was a good honeypot?"

The man called out that he had no intention of ruining his suit by swimming to shore. So Cordelia hurried off to find Archie and Zedediah, who brought down a coil of rope. Jake swam one end of it out to the dock, and the others pulled it back in.

The impostor, still pretending to be an agent of the state, announced as he stepped off the dock onto the shore that the state could shut them down immediately on the basis of the pond alone. But when he noticed Harley taking pictures, he went suddenly silent and allowed himself to be escorted back to the dining tent, glancing over his shoulder every few steps at Winston, who was trotting along behind him, alternately growling and whuffling all the way. Sybil, Lucille, and Randolph met the procession, and Paulie, who'd been moved out of the kitchen and into the tent, greeted them all with his usual cascade of curses and then demanded a peanut.

It wasn't until Lucille and Sybil had seated him at a picnic table and Harley announced he was going to the office to upload the photographs he'd taken of the "rescue" at the pond that Thomas Timmons broke down and admitted that he was neither Thomas Timmons nor an agent of the state.

Randolph threatened to call the police on the spot.

"No one's had breakfast yet," Sybil protested. "It's never good to make important decisions on an empty stomach!"

"There's no decision to be made!" Randolph said. "This person has perpetrated a fraud! I guarantee you there's a law about impersonating a government employee and terrorizing innocent citizens! He is a criminal, and it's our *duty* to turn him over to the authorities!"

"He's not *going* anywhere, Randolph," Zedediah said. "Breakfast first, authorities later. I for one would like to hear the young man's story before we send him off to jail."

Lucille smiled beatifically. "Think of it this way, Randolph. Terror can be an excellent motivator. Just go inside and look at the kitchen. It's absolutely sparkling. I don't think the refrigerator has *ever* been so clean!"

"And now we know why," Sybil added. "Cleaning a refrigerator is an appalling job!"

So it was decided that everyone who needed to would shower and change and gather back in the dining tent for breakfast, while Lucille and Harley printed out the pictures Harley had taken—pictures, Randolph reminded the impostor, that would serve as evidence of fraud in a court of law.

When breakfast was over, the interrogation of the prisoner began.

"My name is Jonathon Sandler," he said, surrendering his fake ID badge. "I live in Traybridge. I'm an actor."

"An actor?" Randolph scoffed. "There's no work for an actor in Traybridge!"

"You're telling me! That's why I went to New York right out of college. I tried my luck there for three years and only managed to get two roles in all that time—both of them off-off-Broadway. No money. I survived as a bookkeeping temp."

Zedediah, who had been sitting next to Destiny watching him draw possums on a sketch pad, looked up. "Were you any good at it?"

"I got a couple of pretty good reviews—"

"I meant at bookkeeping!"

"Oh. Everybody I did temp work for wanted to hire me full-time. But I wanted to stay free to take whatever acting job came along. A lot of good that did me. I finally just gave up and came home. I figured even if Traybridge Little Theatre didn't pay, I could at least get onstage there. When I went to audition, Mrs. Montrose offered me this job instead."

Randolph erupted in fury. "This *job*? It isn't an acting job; it's a criminal conspiracy! Call the police *now*! We can get that wretched woman on conspiracy to defraud! I knew all along she had to be behind this."

Jonathon Sandler, scratching his neck, grinned sheepishly. "She offered to pay really well!"

When the whole story came out, it was pretty much

what E.D. had suspected. When Mrs. Montrose couldn't get the state interested in *Eureka!*, she'd decided to get revenge on the Applewhites as best she could.

"It was to be a kind of terrorist action at first," Sandler explained. "The intention was to inflict psychological trauma. So she had me deliver all those messages about the state regulations day after day. Then I was supposed to let myself get seen skulking around. She didn't warn me about the goat! I wouldn't have come back after that horrible day, but the goat tore the suit. It was from the costume shop at the Little Theatre, and she told me she'd take the cost of it out of my pay. I had to come back to earn the rest of it or I'd have ended up in debt!"

"She intended to inflict psychological trauma?" Randolph said. "When the case comes to trial, she'll discover that it didn't work. Applewhites are made of stronger stuff!"

Right, E.D. thought, remembering the look on her father's face the morning she'd seen him with one of Mrs. Montrose's threatening messages crumpled in his hand.

"After the inspection she was planning to forge a 'cease and desist' order from the state—and send it by mail from Raleigh. She thought you'd shut yourselves down to avoid prosecution."

"Never!" Randolph insisted. "We would have fought the state to the last breath!"

E.D. explained the policy of distraction and delay then, and told Jonathon Sandler she was sorry Wolfie had ruined the suit.

Cordelia, who was sitting across the table from him, said, "I hope he didn't hurt you!"

Sandler smiled at her and shook his head. "He scared the devil out of me, though. The worst part wasn't the goat." He scratched at his neck. "It's the poison ivy I got in the woods. It started on my neck, and it's spread all down my back!" Cordelia patted his other hand comfortingly.

Destiny looked up from his drawing pad. "Tell 'em about the Heffalump trap, E.D.!"

She explained about her call to the department. "So we knew you couldn't be a real inspector."

"You *knew*?" Randolph said. "You knew and didn't tell your family? How sharper than a serpent's tooth . . ."

David pointed a finger at Sandler. "I suggested capture and torture. You're lucky everybody else here is such a wimp."

"Then I had a Pooh and Piglet idea!" Destiny crowed. "The dock was a Heffalump trap, and I was the honeypot! And it worked! We caught you!"

"Yeah. You caught me." Sandler breathed a long, shuddery sigh. "And now I'll never get the rest of my pay. I'm back to being a starving artist!"

"You're going to jail—that's what's going to happen

to you! Don't think for one minute that we won't bring the full force of the law down on your head. And on the head of that vengeful, sadistic woman!" Randolph turned to Lucille. "You printed out those pictures, didn't you? They'll be all the evidence we need."

Lucille held up Harley's photographs. "They're evidence, all right. But we're not going to turn them over to the authorities."

"What do you mean? Of course we are!" Randolph said.

"There is a Higher Authority involved here, Randolph," she said. "Take a look." She spread the photos on the table. In almost every one of them, orbs could be seen clustered around Jonathon Sandler's head. "There. You see? Orbs! Benevolent spirits, drawn to light and joy. They would not be in these photographs if this young man had come here with malicious intent. He is here for some higher purpose—a higher purpose than Mrs. Montrose could ever have imagined."

"And what," Randolph asked with acid in his voice, "might that purpose be exactly?"

"It will emerge in time," Lucille said blithely. "You may be sure of that."

"It may have emerged already," Zedediah said. "Zedediah Applewhite Handmade Wood Furniture is in serious need of a bookkeeper. I've been working overtime, and I can't keep up with the books. For that matter, this whole family would benefit from having somebody around who knows how to keep track of money."

"Now *there's* a good idea!" Sybil said.

"I do have a degree in accounting," Jonathon said. "Of course, I really prefer acting. . . ."

"It's possible," Sybil said, "that there will be a place for you in one of Randolph's productions from time to time."

"Are you *kidding?*" Randolph said. "After all he's done . . ."

"Well, the least you could do is let him audition, dear," Sybil said. "As well as he played the part of Thomas Timmons, he could turn out to be a real asset!"

Jonathon Sandler was smiling. E.D. noticed that Cordelia hadn't moved her hand from his since she'd patted it.

Sandler looked up at Randolph. "It would be an honor to be in a Randolph Applewhite production," he said.

"There now! All's well that ends well," Lucille said. "The whole point of *Eureka!* is to nourish creativity in these children, and look how creative they've been. Look how brilliantly they worked together to save the camp."

"It was never actually in danger," Randolph pointed out.

Zedediah stood up and swept his arm around the dining tent where the breakfast dishes were drawing flies and yellow jackets. "Who has KP for Community Service? The day is getting away from us. We still have a camp to run, after all!"

Chapter Thirty-six

"It seems to me," Zedediah said at that night's staff meeting, "that camp, like education, involves an adventurous quest. Kids learn not so much from what they're *taught* as from what they *do*."

"Not just kids," Sybil said. "The more I work on my children's book, the better I get! *Petunia Possum, P.I.* It's going to be a stunner."

"Don't forget magic," Lucille added. "The orbs are with us!"

"Orbs!" Paulie muttered sleepily from his perch. "Orbs, orbs, orbs."

Zedediah rubbed his hands together. "All right, then. You all have another month to encourage these kids to do what they do best—"

"Not *just* what they do best!" E.D. protested.

Jake nodded. "If that's all they do, how will they ever find out the rest of who they are?"

Hal, who almost never spoke up at a staff meeting, cleared his throat. "Like me being a counselor. Doing the hard stuff's what makes it an adventure."

"Focus, focus, focus!" Randolph said. "If we aren't going to prosecute Mrs. Montrose, it's time to get serious about an end-of-camp event that will show her and the whole of Traybridge, North Carolina, what real talent and creativity can do! Theater, dance, music, art. I say we sell tickets and rub her nose in our success!"

"We already have a theme," Lucille said. "The barn's becoming a patchwork quilt. We could make it a whole day of family activities and call it the Patchwork Summer Festival of the Arts. Just imagine it: strolling singers—"

"—storytelling for kids," Sybil added.

"Face painting!" Cordelia said. "And Q can teach people Step!"

Hal nodded. "Art gallery in the barn . . ."

Lucille clapped her hands. "Perfect! A gallery of sculpture and photographs. We can have a whole section just for orbs. We'll have to have food, of course.

Barbecue, hot dogs, fried green tomatoes. I'll see if I can get my guru, Govindaswami, to come and do a booth with Indian food. . . ."

"If Cinnamon has really tamed Wolfie, we could have a petting zoo!" Sybil said.

"And most important," Randolph said, "a show to cap it all off. We'll call it *A Patchwork Evening of Scenes and Improv.*"

"Don't forget New Fusion Movement—that's what we've decided to call it—ballet, Step, tap, and modern dance," Cordelia put in. "Jonathon told me he studied dance the whole time he was in New York. He could be in it too!"

"Sybil and I will start organizing the publicity tomorrow!" Lucille said. "It'll be a sellout."

Jake looked at E.D.; E.D. looked at Jake. Both of them sighed.

Archie, who had offered to watch the campers during the staff meeting, had built a campfire and gathered them all for a marshmallow roast to celebrate *Eureka!*'s reprieve from the state. He sent Samantha to the Lodge to invite the staff to join them after the meeting.

Jake and E.D. stood together, leaning on the porch rail, after the others had gone out to the campfire circle. Winston had settled next to them, chin on his paws.

"They're off again, aren't they?" Jake asked.

252

E.D. looked up at Jake's face, lit by the full moon. When had he gotten so much taller, she wondered. And why hadn't she noticed? His Mohawk had begun to tip over, softening his old delinquent look. The ring in his eyebrow glittered in the moonlight. "There's nothing like the passion of the Applewhites," she said.

"You ought to know," Jake said. "You *are* one." He grinned. "That was some act you put on today."

Jake thought back to the first time he'd seen her— not even a whole year ago. She'd had scabby elbows and knees then, chopped-off hair, and a body like a ten-year-old boy. And she had clearly hated him. The feeling, he remembered, had been mutual.

The sound of Archie's guitar floated up to them from the campfire. After a moment Harley and Ginger began to sing Ginger's latest song. "Moonlight on the water, mockingbird in the trees, come and join the laughter caught on the evening breeze. . . ." An owl hooted from the woods.

They could never say later whether E.D. had kissed Jake or Jake had kissed E.D., but Winston's tail thumped on the porch floor. Even the dog knew how much had changed.